JESSIE HAAS

CHASE

SCHOLASTIC INC.
New York Toronto London Auckland Sydney
Mexico City New Delhi Hong Kong Buenos Aires

ISBN-13: 978-0-545-10158-5
ISBN-10: 0-545-10158-1

12 11 10 9 8 7 6 5 4 3 2 1   8 9 10 11 12 13/0

Printed in the U.S.A.   40

First Scholastic printing, October 2008

The text of this book is set in Aldine 401.
Book design by Sylvie Le Floc'h

For the Monday Night Group: Pam Becker, Erica Breen,
Jay Callahan, Michael J. Daley, John Steven Gurney,
Erin Heidorn, Andra Horton, J. D. McNeil,
Rose-Marie Provencher, Jean Rice Shaw, Jeanne Walsh,
and the late Seth Wheeler

and for Rebecca Davis

CONTENTS

1
ENGELBREIT

Phin surfaced from the book with a start and sat listening; for what, he wasn't sure.

It was hours later, the lamp pale and unneeded, the sky blue, with a glowing red-orange streak at the horizon. Engelbreit was sleeping late this morning. Dawn usually found him up and breakfasting, then off to the mine to meet the incoming shift. In these troubled times it was best to be on hand early, to smell out whatever mischief had brewed overnight.

But Engelbreit was only just stirring in his blankets. That must be the sound that had startled Phin. Then why was he still listening? Why was he thinking of his mother?

He glanced down at the great poem he'd been so deep in moments ago. They'd never shared *Leaves of Grass*. It was two weeks after her death that he'd discovered Engelbreit and his books.

There were twenty-two of them on the shelf next to the table. Four had to do with coal and engineering, but there were novels, history, and poetry, too. Engelbreit wouldn't loan them. He'd caught Phin reading a novel left on the bench outside his door. "Come anytime," he'd said. "If I'm asleep, don't wake me. Just light the lamp and read."

For ten months now Phin had come almost every night. It felt more like home than the empty room behind Murray's Tavern. He missed her less here, and more. *Isn't this beautiful?* he kept wanting to ask her; or *What do you think?* And he'd look up from the page and remember.

But this wasn't one of those times. He didn't feel sorrowful, just—uneasy.

He leaned to blow out the lamp as Engelbreit rose, shoved his feet into his boots, and opened the front door wide. The sun was just coming up.

Engelbreit went out, dipped water from the barrel, and washed his face and hands. He came back in, leaving the door open. It was early autumn. The breeze brought a spicy smell from beyond the coalfields.

2. CHASE

"Do you ever sleep, boy?" He rubbed his palms over his face; broad, bearded, maned like a lion. His calm blue eyes looked curiously at Phin, who shrugged. Sleep was hard to come by at a saloon. Sometimes he slept in the early morning, when things got quiet, or he'd slip away to the stable and bed down in the hay. Engelbreit didn't know that, and he didn't know much about Engelbreit. What they spoke of when they got the chance was books, and they didn't get the chance often.

Engelbreit drove his men like a demon, so the talk ran at Murray's. Phin had seen him come home, this demon, as soaked with sweat as any black-faced miner; throw himself on the bed and lie there wide-eyed, too exhausted to sleep. He'd seen him at his figures, shaking his head. The numbers didn't come out right. Working like a demon wasn't enough, for him or anyone else these days.

Engelbreit bent to kindle a fire in the stove. The sun struck a golden spear through the doorway. "Have some breakfast, since you're here?"

Just then a shadow crossed the sunbeam on the floor, then two more shadows. Shoulders. Hats. Like dark dolls the shapes lengthened over the clean-swept boards. Phin looked around.

Ned Plume came first, walking straight to the door with

a revolver in his hand. He carried it down by his side, casual as a man with a dinner pail. He was tall and straight and his shoulders swung easily. The two behind were nervous and had been drinking.

There was time for one word. "Sleepers," Phin said, and Engelbreit turned from his breakfast.

Turned slowly. It was already too late. His eyes were fearless, and Plume raised the gun and fired. Red blossomed on Engelbreit's shirt and he fell back. When his head struck the iron stove, the look in his eyes didn't change. He was already gone.

Phin had seen dead men. In coal country in 1875, you did.

But Engelbreit. The sun through the open doorway, bright rose of red on his shirt. Engelbreit's calm eyes—

The next shot would slam into Phin. He refused to turn and see it. Engelbreit's face would be his last sight on earth—

Footsteps, a rustle of clothing. Hands grabbed his upper arms, hard and hot as iron from the forge. He was jerked around to face Ned Plume.

The morning light gilded Plume's face. He looked handsome and noble, like a dime-novel hero, as he raised his gun again.

Phin swooped out of his body to a high corner of the ceiling. He saw the gun leveled at him, a shabby boy with a mended tear in the top of his cap. The boy looked calm, as detached as Engelbreit. Plume squared his jaw, squared it again, and his knuckle whitened on the trigger.

Abruptly he dropped his gun hand to his side. "This one I can't do."

Phin fell back into his body, a shrinking prison of fear. "He knows something," said the man holding him. " 'Sleepers,' he said."

But everyone knew the Sleepers. You pretended not to, but you did. And working at Murray's—an Irish tavern, in an Irish mine town—you'd have to be blind and deaf not to. The Sleepers—Molly Maguires, Ancient Order of Hibernians, to give them their other names—were the Irish defense force. Or they were a band of thugs; opinion was divided, even among the Irish.

Phin knew about the secret passwords and handshakes; about the coffin notices, threats with black coffins drawn on them to scare off oppressive bosses. He knew about the body masters who headed each local group. He knew about the gunmen. But everyone was aware of those things. He'd known everything, and nothing; certainly nothing worth dying for, until now.

"You do it," Plume said. The hands holding Phin jerked. Plume laughed. "Not so easy, is it? But here's a plan—"

"Who is the kid?" a voice outside asked.

"Mary Chase's boy. Works for Murray," Plume said. "English."

"Mary was Irish, I thought."

"The father was English."

"No matter," Plume said. "Didn't we walk in here, boys—to discuss our legitimate grievances!—and find Engelbreit dead and this lad tossing the place!" As he spoke, Plume moved casually through the little room, yanking open a drawer and scooping out the clothing, kicking over a chair. "No one more shocked than ourselves, mind"—he cleared the books from the shelf in one long sweep—"and we restrained ourselves from stringing him up, and decided we'd turn him over to the constable."

A Sleeper. The constable was a Sleeper.

"Engelbreit was liked upstairs," said the voice outside the door. "Lot of vigilante talk. Maybe the lad won't live till his trial."

"Maybe not." Plume turned toward the door. "Bring him. They've ignored the shot as long as they can, on the Street. They're coming."

The iron hands loosened, shifting to grip the back of Phin's jacket.

Phin didn't think, just twisted out of the loose-fitting garment and dived across the table. He kicked the book and the lamp fell and he went through the window, finding his feet while glass still clinked to the ground. Around the corner, tearing the window sash off his neck. A shot. Another—

His legs pumped and his loose shirt flapped against his ribs. Wind droned in his ears, a hollow sound like a set of pipes. Faster than he'd ever run, but it felt slow. He saw everything clearly, as if with his whole body, not just his eyes. A pigpen built of fresh slabs; the pitch dripped like honey, glistening in the sunlight. A woman threw a basin of water out her back door in a gleaming pewter arc. Did he touch the ground, even? He didn't feel his feet, didn't feel anything or fully snap into his body again, until he reached the yard of Murray's Tavern.

Two habitual drunks snored in their habitual corners. Duff Murray stood in the doorway, scratching his bristled jowl and then scratching under his shirt. His eyes were small and red-rimmed, and blinked resentfully at the sun.

Phin half fell to a stop. He'd come here because it was

home, but it was the wrong place. He turned his head, ready to run. Murray's big hand shot out, swift as a frog snapping a fly, and caught him by the shirt.

"Wood," he said. "Wash." As well as spirits and games of chance, Murray's offered rooms and breakfasts and clothes laundered, a dozen useful ways for a boy to earn his keep.

Phin tried to speak. His dry lips couldn't form the words. He licked them with a dry tongue.

"They shot him!"

"Engelbreit." Murray's red eyes were unmoving. "How does that concern me?"

Fear congealed like cold grease around Phin's bones. He hadn't said who was shot, but Murray knew.

"They—" he said.

Murray said nothing.

"They'll—swear it off on me. I'll hang."

Murray's face didn't change. "You were where you didn't belong, boy. Else how would you know about it."

The heap of clothing in the corner near the door stirred. That was Jim Kane, who by afternoon would be up and sauntering around, bright-eyed, and who by evening could dance a jig and sing a tune with the best of them, until he collapsed again about two in the morning. Usually he slept till noon, but their voices were disturbing him.

When he awoke, he'd see Phin—and Jim Kane would sell anything to anyone for the price of a drink.

"Please," Phin said.

The ugly face didn't soften, but the grip on Phin's shirt slowly did. "One favor," Murray said finally. "For your mother's memory. I haven't seen you." He spun Phin around as lightly as he'd spin a glass onto the bar, and twitched him free.

2
WIDOW'S ROW

He'd run the breath out of his body, the bones out of his legs. He stumbled around the corner, blundered into a fence, leaned there, heaving for breath, trying to hear above the blood pounding in his ears.

The ground shook; a charge going off underground. The shift had started work—so they didn't know yet. That meant Mahoney didn't know, either. The Sleeper constable always managed to be below when Sleeper mischief was afoot.

Phin pushed off from the fence, driving himself on, past plank houses, plank fences, bare dirt yards and scrubby trees, a back garden, a tethered goat—

"Phin?"

A woman's voice. He stopped, legs braced wide to hold himself up, and turned blindly.

"Phin Chase, what are you up to?" Beautiful red-haired Margaret Wimsy stood at the doorway of her cabin, fastening up a morning glory vine. "Come here!" she said.

He heard hoofbeats now, distant but coming this way. He wanted to run, *must* run. Yet he walked toward Margaret through the syrupy, resistant air. His head felt an immense distance from his feet.

"Take this to Murray's for me, will you?" She handed him a package, wrapped in newspaper and tied with a piece of tired ribbon. "Tell Murray put it in a safe place." Turning back to her flowers, she spoke over her shoulder. "A fine, careless man, Ned Plume, but he'd skin a flea for its hide and tallow. Must have a lot on his mind this morning, leaving his wallet here!"

His wallet.

Plume's wallet.

Fear-sweat dampened Phin's face. He ducked his head to hide it. Did she know what Plume had on his mind? *Could* she know, and handle her flowers so carelessly?

Her voice came as if from a distance. "Tell Ned I said you're to have a penny for your trouble. Put that away now. Don't carry it out in the open."

No. Not out in the open. Phin slid the package into his pocket.

"Cool morning to go without a jacket, Phinny!"

He risked a glance at her face. Not motherly, Margaret, but she'd been his mother's friend, and she looked out for him, though it didn't come naturally. A moment more and she'd notice the state he was in. He turned numbly, and heard her close her door.

Was the wallet full of money? Did she care?

She might not. Like a queen out of the old tales, Margaret Wimsy did as she liked. Drank at Murray's; decent women didn't. Chose her own man, and chose again if another pleased her better. Last year when Ned Plume came to Bittsville, he became Margaret's at once. Phin remembered the clash of their eyes across the smoky room, the challenge flung down and accepted. They were like a pair of eagles—nothing soft about their love. "There must be more to him than meets the eye," Phin's mother had said. "She's no fool, Margaret—but I still think she could do better." Maybe, but not here in coal country. Ned Plume was top Sleeper gunman. His belongings were safe anywhere in Bittsville; no one would filch so much as a cigarette paper.

Phin had his whole wallet.

The thought kicked him forward in a wavering run, angling among the fences and back sheds, ever farther from the Street. The ground boomed and jumped beneath him, the breaker growled, and under those sounds came the hoofbeats, closer, slowing as if they were right among the houses. Phin swerved uphill, into the narrow lane of Widow's Row, forcing himself to walk.

Here the morning was loud with goats and babies, women talking, children shouting. The houses were tiny and leaned toward each other in a gossipy way across rickety fences. Miners' widows and orphans lived here. During the war, when he was small, Phin and his mother had too.

His father was still alive then, but he'd been marched away with six other Bittsville miners, to fight in a Union regiment. For two years Phin's mother waited. Then one day she told Nan Lundy, "He'll not come home."

"You've heard nothing."

"I've heard." She'd had a hundred nightmares about him, she said, and then one quiet little dream like a telegram that she knew was true. And it must have been, because he never did come back.

The hoofbeats were louder. Phin glanced over his shoulder. The houses blocked his view. Hopefully that worked both ways. He pulled his cap down and hurried on. Though he was vaguely aware of women in doorways, no one called his name. When his mother moved to Murray's, where she could feed her boy on what she earned as a laundress, keep him out of the breaker and the mine, she'd lost most of her respectable friends. Too young, too pretty, to go live in a saloon. Even if she'd been a toothless crone, it would have been a little scandalous. Only Nan Lundy was left, down on her luck these days and living here, in the last shack in Widow's Row, behind the flimsiest gate.

Phin pushed through and shut it behind him, and his legs took a running step all on their own. Just one. There were eyes everywhere, even here in the Lundys' yard. Walk.

The door stood open, daylight being cheaper than lamp oil. Mr. Lundy sat in his chair, knife flashing steadily as he carved a continuous chain out of an ash log. Phin blundered up the path, half falling. Lundy lifted his round dark eyes.

Don't, the eyes said. *Don't bring trouble to this house.*

The clear, silent message shocked Phin awake. Lundy'd been crippled in the mine. With six children to support, his wife wore herself out washing other men's clothes. Phin couldn't add to their burden.

Anyway, hadn't the AOH given the Lundys money, after the accident? The Ancient Order of Hibernians—respectable, legal, organized for charity and to protect Irish rights—and connected some way with the Sleepers. Phin had to be careful even here.

"I'm leaving." His words surprised him. Inside, Mrs. Lundy turned from her enormous heap of laundry. "I stopped to say good-bye."

"And where, so sudden?" Nan Lundy came out, drying her reddened hands on her apron. "D'you have someone to go to? Did Mary's relatives write?"

It was an old dream of his mother's—the letter, and him walking east and taking ship to Ireland. He should see it, his mother said, and England, too, choose for himself, not just stick to the choices his parents had made. Her uncle would come into money someday, and then it might be possible to live in Ireland.

Mrs. Lundy opened her mouth, took a quick breath as she tried to marshall her questions. Then she glanced sharply at Phin and went to stand by her husband's chair, putting one hand on his shoulder.

Lundy's slow eyes looked Phin up, looked him down. No coat. No bundle. Shirt thin and ragged, breath coming hard, and whatever showed on his face. Phin had no idea what that was. His mouth felt like it was smiling and his back prickled. He kept twisting to glance over his shoulder—

"Step inside," Lundy said. "That piece of bacon, Nan. And cold biscuit—haven't we got some cold biscuit?"

"Just—" She didn't finish. Just that for your dinner, is what she would have said.

"Matches," said Lundy. "On a journey like that, you'll want matches." He reached down beside his chair and brought up one of the many cylindrical boxes he had carved.

His wife counted out the precious matchsticks, hesitated, her hand hovering over the box, then hastily added two more. Just so she and Phin's mother used to help each other, giving greatly on washerwomen's earnings.

Lundy unfastened the bandanna from his neck. His wife tied it around the biscuits, the matchbox, and a small lump of bacon she'd cut off a not-much-larger chunk. She gave Phin the bundle.

"Cut yourself a stick when you get out into the country-side," Lundy said. "Got a knife, do you?"

Quickly, so he'd be believed, Phin nodded, glancing over his shoulder again. The Lundys had just one knife. She'd borrowed it from him to cut the bacon.

"Wish you had a bottle for water," Mrs. Lundy said.

"You'll get thirsty, walking. But Jimmy's got all his father's kit now."

Jimmy Lundy, swallowed underground; his little brothers swallowed into the breaker building, picking slate out of anthracite coal. If only Phin had been swallowed, too. If only he'd been safe underground this morning.

Dogs barked near the Street, as if at an intruder. Lundy jerked his head toward the back room. It had no door to the outside, but the window was wide open, letting in air and mosquitoes.

Mrs. Lundy darted ahead of Phin and came back carrying Mikkeleen, the littlest boy, pressing his face into her neck so he couldn't see, couldn't tell. "Go," she mouthed, and leaned to kiss Phin, a hard, dry brush against his cheek. She turned away as Mikkeleen squirmed sleepily.

Phin slipped into the back room and was reaching for the windowsill when a sound froze him—metal striking stone. Mikkeleen said, "Horsie?"

Phin turned around. Mrs. Lundy stood in the front doorway with Mikkeleen in her arms, filling it, blocking the light.

"I can't come to the gate," she said loudly. "The child's sick, and my husband as well." Her tone held the rider at a distance. A little distance; it was a little yard.

"Did a boy come this way?" The voice seemed familiar, but Phin couldn't place it. His life was full of men's voices, calling for drinks or a fresh pack of cards.

Nan Lundy said, "What would a boy be doing abroad, and the sun up already?" The Irish way; answer a question with a question, and you've told no lie. But who could she be talking to?

The man at the gate said, "This boy killed John Engelbreit, the supervisor. Or so they say."

Her back went rigid. She glanced down at her husband. He nodded, jaw jutting. "We heard shots," he said in a carrying voice. "What boy?"

"Chase, I think? Works in Murray's."

Who *was* that? The voice was at once familiar and unknown—like the whole world, this morning. Reality slipping; the way land went liquid beneath your feet when it was undermined.

"What's your interest?" Mr. Lundy asked.

"Murder's everybody's interest, isn't it? I was told the lad came this way."

Lundy sat unmoving. From the shadowed inner room, Phin saw his profile and the bulk of his shoulder, edged with light.

"I was told wrong, then?"

"It would seem that way, wouldn't it?"

"How do I get up on that hill behind the houses? Is there a trail through here?"

"And why would you be wanting to ride on that hill at all?" Lundy asked. "Can the beast fly, that you'd risk him falling down one of those holes?"

"He can about fly, right enough," the man said. A laugh warmed his voice, and for a second Phin almost knew him. "But thanks for the advice."

The dogs took up their barking again. The children began to shout. As the hoofbeats receded, Phin gripped his bundle in his teeth, scrambled up the wall, and eeled through the window into the blackberry and goldenrod. He was running before he hit the ground.

Mistake. He knew it, but couldn't stop himself. Brambles caught him, clawed and slashed and whipped, but he tore through them, wanting only to get away, far away—

Black yawned under him and his foot came down on nothing, down and down and down.

3
THE DOG HOLE

His cheek itched.

He raised his head—tried to raise his head. Stuck to the floor.

Floor? Ground.

He opened his eyes and saw only darkness, something dim and white at a level with his face.

Was he blind? Or was it night? Or—what? He heard nothing, just a faint ringing in his ears. He wasn't at Murray's, then. Always noise there, even if it was just snoring.

He tried again, and his cheek peeled away from whatever he lay on, with a sticky, jammy sensation. His head swam. He wanted to lay it back down, but what was that stuff? He pushed more upright—

Something wrong with his arm. Left arm. Wouldn't push. Felt like an interruption halfway down. Going to hurt soon. In the center of his head, a spinning blankness. He might vomit, or faint.

Where was he?

He remembered running. Man on a horse—what man? Couldn't picture him—

Because he'd never seen him. Voice at the gate—that was all, and he'd fled uphill through the brambles. Not smart, with all the holes—

Holes. He looked up, way up, and there was sky, a small blue patch of it rimmed with blackberry leaves.

His stomach whirled. He braced his good hand on the rock floor, and slowly, because quick movement hurt his head, looked down again.

The white thing—he stared at it a long time, while the lattice shape of it slowly became apparent. Knowing crept from the corners of his mind.

He was in the Dog Hole.

Engelbreit was dead, and he'd been running, and he'd fallen into the Dog Hole.

The countryside for miles around was riddled with

holes—abandoned shafts, wildcat bores. Men went hunting in pairs, so if one fell in, the other could maybe get him out.

This hole up in the briars was well known. A couple of years ago, picking berries, Phin had heard whimpering, looked in, and seen a dog. The mule boys were just knocking off for the day. He'd found Jimmy Lundy, who scrounged a rope, and they argued about who should go down. In the end it was Phin. Jimmy was stronger and should be on top to anchor.

Phin had hated the dark closing around him, the smell of rock and root. A long drop; he remembered that, remembered knowing with every slither and catch down the rope that the dog must be hurt badly.

It lay on its side. He poured a little water from Jimmy's bottle into his cupped hand and offered it. The dog lapped twice. Then, before Phin could touch it, find out what was hurt, it stretched its legs and stopped moving.

They'd left it there, after some shouting. "What good's a dead dog?" Jimmy said finally, ending the argument. They could only bury it, and it was buried deep already. Now so was Phin.

A wave rose from the soles of his feet through every bone and muscle. It emerged a whisper: "Help."

He took a breath to really shout and a thought came, clear and distinct as someone else's voice.

Don't.

He eased the breath out. That's right. Don't panic. Panic got him into this mess; a bad situation, but he could make it worse. Someone was hunting him. If he shouted, it might be that person who heard.

His swimming head slowly settled. Distantly, his body ached. He wondered how badly he was hurt, and patted himself over with his right hand.

Lump on the left forearm, big through his shirt. He only touched it lightly. If it was broken, he didn't want to know. Break or bruise, it left his hand numb. His arm ached from wrist to shoulder.

His face was sticky down the right side. That was blood, from a gash above his hairline. How long had it taken for his own blood to dry and stick him to the floor?

The fingers of his right hand stung. A nail was torn. He must have hit the side of the hole, maybe grabbed the edge. Slowed his fall. That must be why he wasn't dead.

Yet.

He couldn't keep that thought back, but the wild clamor of fear didn't reawaken. He drew a long breath, one that seemed to fill him with something more than air. Keeping his eyes on the scrap of sky, he pushed his feet against the ground, slid his back up and up the wall of the Dog Hole until he was standing.

He didn't vomit. Good. A little dizzy, but that passed after a moment. He turned to the unseen wall and felt along it with his good hand. It was rough and crumbly, with embedded stones, and holes where other stones had fallen out, leaving little crevices. One sloping socket was big enough for a handhold.

Now find another.

His left arm told him it couldn't reach up. Not over his head.

Marking the location of the first handhold in his mind, Phin reluctantly let go of it. A bit farther over he found a small crack where fingers could cling. He grasped his left wrist, and lifted the hand up, up—

Oh it hurt.

Tears released hot down his cold face. His breath came in sobs. With his right hand he jammed the fingers of his left into the little crack. The cold gravel felt distant—

Above him a horse's shod hoof struck stone.

Phin pressed his face to the wall of the Dog Hole and stood unmoving. His breath stopped, and his tears did, too. It was dark down here. In dark clothes, under dark hair, he should be invisible.

The wall he'd thought he couldn't see blackened perceptibly. Someone had shadowed the hole, was looking in.

"Phe-e-e-ew!" Half voice, half whistle; a man admitting he was scared or otherwise impressed. The horse stamped and snorted. Perhaps it had warned him of the hole. Perhaps he'd tried to force it on, and been unable. Horses sensed things humans didn't—

The wall brightened again. A few crumbles of dirt pattered on Phin's head. After a bit the hoof sound came again, turning, going away.

Phin waited a long time before moving. He hadn't heard the horse coming. How did he know it was really gone?

And who could be hunting him on horseback? Mahoney, the constable, was a miner, and miners didn't ride in Bittsville. They walked.

It had been quiet a long time now. Time to try again.

His left hand still clung, numbly, to the crack. Phin groped his way back to the first handhold, clawed his fingers firmly into it.

Now—walk his feet up. Hang there. Find new handholds, walk again. Simple.

Except only his right hand held, and that for just a

moment. Then it, too, slipped out of its shallow niche and he fell on his back on the floor beside the dog bones.

He lay there half stunned, wanting to scream for the unknown horseman to come back, get him out—kill him, even, as long as it was out under the sky. This wouldn't work. He'd never—

No.

Sit up.

Was this his cap, this soft thing under his hand?

Yes. How fortunate. Everything was going to be all right. Finding his cap was a sign of that. He settled it on his head. It hurt where he'd cut himself, but the extra warmth felt good.

He stood up. He stepped to the wall again. With his right hand, he began to feel his way along. He'd go all the way around the hole like this. He'd assess the whole surface. He'd find better handholds, make his left hand work, climb up. He had to, so he would.

Blindly he began, and blindly he went on. The surface of the hole was fairly uniform. It had a couple of bulges— or maybe just one, he started to worry. Maybe he'd been around once already and was starting again. Hard to tell when all he could see was the little sky above and the blur of dog bones.

A bulge again. This was at least the third time. Despair flooded him, and he dropped his forehead against the outcropping. After all his mother had done to keep him out of the mine, he was going to die underground—

Pebbles rained down on his back.

"*Ssss!*"

Phin didn't move.

"Phin! You down there?"

He knew that voice! He stepped back, looked up, and saw a round head against the blue. "Jimmy?"

4

JIMMY

Jimmy sagged back, shaking his head. "'Out the back window,' they said, and 'Dog Hole,' said I. But I didn't believe it! *Mikkeleen* wouldn't fall in the Dog Hole!"

Phin didn't say anything. He couldn't. The world above was real again, and fear was real, too.

"How bad you hurt?" Jimmy asked. "Can you climb a rope?"

Phin swallowed. "I . . . don't think so."

"I can't haul you up," Jimmy said. "It's a dead drop."

"Ladder?"

Jimmy ignored him. "If I knot it? Could you climb a rope with knots?"

It sounded impossible. "I think so."

"I'll get one," Jimmy scrambled to his feet, then leaned down again with a sardonic grin. "Don't go anywhere!"

Phin sagged against the wall. Jimmy. Of course. He couldn't get himself out. Jimmy Lundy could. Wasn't that how it had always been?

They'd been inseparable until age seven, when Jimmy went into the breaker. Phin had waited for his own lunch pail, waited to go to work. When it didn't happen, he asked.

"I need your help here," his mother said. It took him years to see that she was lying.

She wanted him to read to her. Work went easier, she said, with something to think of besides coal-grimed shirts. The books were hard, but she helped him understand what the sentences meant.

"Whoso would be a man must be a noncomformist." That was from "Self Reliance," by Emerson. Phin's father had come to America because of this essay, and had courted his mother by reading it to her. "Whoso" meant whoever, she told him. "Would": wants to be. "A man" was a person grown large, deep, subtle, and strong in character. "Nonconformist": true to yourself, no matter what other people think.

JIMMY · 29

"Are you a man?" Phin asked his mother. She laughed, rare in those years.

"You know, Phin, I believe I am! But don't tell anyone."

He could see her up to her elbows in water, listening as he read. An Irish washerwoman wasn't supposed to read at all, let alone read Emerson. But Mary Chase was free; born that way, kept that way through her own determination. Somebody—who was it?—said about her, "When Mary came to America, she thought it was all for her."

No wonder she defeated Phin—kept him reading, hauling wood and water, while Jimmy graduated to the mine, opening a certain door for ore carts, otherwise watching that it stayed closed, and making up songs to keep himself awake.

Johnny O'Connor became a door boy, too. One day he sang himself to sleep. A cart rumbled into the door, and it flew back and smashed him. It was the kind of thing that happened.

But Jimmy Lundy passed unscathed from door boy to mule boy. Fifteen now, he belonged to a swaggering group of young mine workers. They fought among themselves, swore continually, told jokes Phin didn't understand and stories he could understand but not picture. He'd never been below the surface to see for himself.

He argued with his mother. She'd kept him out of everything exciting and important, and she was so thin these days, so tired. Shouldn't he go to work now, earn money to help out? She could find some girl to read to her.

She straightened from her washboard. Her arms were red and her hands redder, and on her face was an expression he didn't understand, then or now.

"I don't want you getting used to it," she said. "When you're grown you can decide, but you're not grown yet, Phin."

He could have proved her wrong. He could have gone to the mine and taken what work was offered. He didn't because he half understood. She'd moved to Murray's for his sake, and while she didn't mind what people said, she didn't go there because she liked it. If Phin went into the mine, her sacrifice would be for nothing.

So it was Murray's he got used to, the world of drink and gambling, late nights and open secrets. That and the stable, clean and quiet, smelling peacefully of horses. It kept him busy enough that he saw Jimmy only in passing; Jimmy always part of a crowd.

Now Phin realized, staring at the dark wall of the Dog Hole, that he didn't know where Jimmy's loyalties lay. At Murray's he'd watched, eavesdropped, tried to put together the puzzle: who was a union man, who AOH? Who was a Sleeper? Who combined both, or all three? Fascinating, treacherous currents, and he'd watched the surface. Jimmy swam them. Sweat popped out on Phin's brow. Who might Jimmy be talking to, right this minute?

The Sleepers didn't take boys, he was pretty sure; not even mule boys. But Jimmy should be back by now. Shouldn't he be back—

"Tell me when this hits the floor." Jimmy was there again, paying a fat rope down the side of the hole yard by yard.

Every ugly thought of betrayal left Phin instantly. He waited for the rope. "Got it."

"Here's more. The knots'll make it shorter. Holler when you've got ten or twelve extra feet."

There were fifteen extra feet when Phin called up again. The rope was big around as a beer glass. Knots took up more of a thick rope, didn't they? It was the kind of thing Engelbreit would—

No. Don't think about Engelbreit.

Jimmy hauled the rope up. Phin heard low-voiced swearing. It would be hard knotting such a long rope, especially if you wanted to work fast.

Not as hard as it was going to be to climb it.

Phin massaged his left arm. It wasn't broken, but the hand had no strength. He could barely close it, let alone squeeze.

After a few minutes the rope came down again, knot by lumpy knot. Jimmy looked over the edge. "Got it? Let me get set, then. When I twitch, you come ahead."

Get set how? There was no tree up there to wrap the rope around, not even a good-sized rock. How would Jimmy do it? What would he brace against?

Don't think about that. He had his own job to do.

The rope twitched. Phin reached up with his right hand and got a firm grip. With his left forearm, he pinned the rope against his body. He stepped on the first knot—

It wasn't as simple as stepping. His boots slipped and fumbled, and he clamped the rope with his knees, pinched it between the arches of his feet, his whole body gripping it desperately. He drew himself up; one inchworm length, one knot.

The rope wobbled alarmingly. He could fall now and be all right, but for every foot he climbed, the fall would get worse—

"Hurry!" Jimmy's voice reached him in an oddly flattened way. There was no choice. Phin took a deep breath and started up.

Reach. Pin. Worm his feet up, grip the knot, and push. Reach. Pin. Worm and push. Reach, pin . . .

His arches began to ache. His knees felt raw. His arm muscles shook.

Worst of all was the reach, that moment when only his weak left arm hugging the rope kept him from falling. Or maybe the worst was bumping the side of the hole, or the way the rope shuddered and swayed. He didn't look down, did his best not to think. Just count the knots. Eleven. Twelve. Thirteen.

The light got broader and nearer and finally blazed in his eyes, half blinding him. The rope disappeared over the edge of the hole at an angle. Phin reached. His left foot slipped off the knot and kicked the side, setting loose a shower of small stones. They pattered far below. His right hand closed on the unseen rope, and Jimmy said, "That's the boy. Up and at 'em!"

Phin pushed off the last knot, throwing himself over the edge of the hole, scrabbling with toes and knees and elbows.

Sun on his shoulders, a blur of bushes, packed earth under him, and Jimmy twenty feet away braced against a small rock, straining at the rope, a look of horror on his face.

Wasn't he going to make it? Phin scrambled forward and sprawled on his stomach. Jimmy fell back. The rope flew in the air and dived snakelike down the hole, but Jimmy rolled up and over and after it. He caught the tail just in time and turned toward Phin, staring, gradually going green in the face.

"What?" Phin touched his cheek. It was stiff, crusty with dried blood. "I didn't do it," he said quickly.

Jimmy tried to smile. "Right," he said, and swallowed. " 'Phin Chase shoot a man?' I said. 'Next you'll be tellin' me'—ugh!"

He sat down abruptly and put his head between his knees. His hand fumbled inside his shirt, and a moment later he brought out a water flask, untied his bandanna.

"Cripes, Phin, will you wash your face?"

5
DROVE

Phin fumbled the bandanna open to its cleanest surface. He uncorked the bottle, took a long pull, then sloshed water onto the cloth. His hands shook, spilling some on the ground. He bunched the cloth and scrubbed.

Jimmy hauled the rope up. *Slap slap*, it landed in loose coils. *Slap slap* went Jimmy's voice. "Here's the way of it. We downed tools, half of us, when we heard about Engelbreit. They had no call to kill him. So he was a hard driver! I say no man can drive you if you don't let yourself be drove. The men he let go were drinkin' down there. Could have killed any one of us."

Slap slap swish—the end of the rope emerged in

sunlight. Jimmy started to pull apart the first knot. "So there's more men out than you'd think, this time of day. That's one thing."

"What about . . . Plume?"

Jimmy glanced over his shoulder at Phin. He was pale under the coal dust. His thin black eyebrows looked like the wings of distant birds. "Plume came down late and stayed down. Don't tell me, Phin. I don't even want to guess!"

Wise. Guessing could get you killed.

"Constable's at Dennis's," Jimmy said. "Saw him when I nicked the rope. 'Did you look at Murray's,' Dennis says. 'Murray hasn't seen him,' says Mahoney. He's searching the barn now, so I say go there."

"What?"

"Time you get there, he'll be gone. He won't look again for a while."

Phin shook his head, trying to get his brain started. That was good thinking, hide-and-seek thinking—what he needed to start doing—but he was still stupid with shock.

"Okay," he said. "Then what?"

Jimmy looked full at him. His eyes were startlingly like his father's, round and dark and heavy. "Get down to the yard tonight, hop a freight. Don't stop till you're out of coal country."

Phin stared. Out of Bittsville, he'd been thinking—but Jimmy was right. Wherever anthracite and Irish came together, you'd find Sleepers; Coal and Iron Police, too, the private army raised by the mine companies.

Away from Irish, then. Away from mines—away from all of this, exactly as his mother had wanted.

But he'd always thought he'd leave freely, not be driven. "Why should I run?" he said. "I didn't do it."

"Don't be simple, Phin! You can't go to the owners— they think you killed Engelbreit! The union's smashed— anyway, you were never a miner. And the AOH—well, you aren't Irish, are you? And they're so thick with the other crowd, you might as well turn yourself in at the jailhouse as go to them."

Jail? Phin could feel the bars closing around him—and that was bad, but it would be shelter. Would he be allowed even that much? "Vigilantes—they said—"

"Wouldn't take vigilantes to settle your hash. All it'd take is the right jury!"

Phin knew that was true. The word would be passed, the verdict predetermined; and would Bittsville do that to him? A harmless boy?

It would. He was caught in something big—caught but left out, too, not securely part of any one group.

He nodded. Yes. Yes, he'd go.

"Your parents—did they tell you about the rider?" he asked. "Who was he?"

"They didn't know him. C'mon." Jimmy helped Phin to his feet. Phin straightened; Jimmy pushed him, making him stagger. "Get ahold of yourself, Phinny, or you're done for!"

Oh. Stay low. Downhill was the Street. Anyone could be looking up.

Jimmy scooped something off the ground—the bundle his parents had given Phin. "Found this behind the house," he said, pushing it into Phin's hands. "Look—" For a moment his glittering, narrowed eyes searched Phin's. "You grew up in the worst dive in Bittsville. You're tougher than this, right? You'll be okay?"

Phin felt himself nodding.

Jimmy gave him a light punch on the shoulder. "Up with ye, Phin! I gotta get back."

And he was gone, the brambles waving behind him.

"Thanks," Phin said, too late.

He put the bundle inside his shirt and turned away, circling wide around the Dog Hole, around the horse tracks with their eloquent, deep-dug rims.

What horse? What rider? Where were they now? Hurry;

but watch for holes. He was tougher than this. Right? His head throbbed, his arm throbbed, something in his pocket thumped his leg at every step—

Plume's wallet.

He'd actually forgotten it. There were blank spots in his mind, like the blank spot his foot came down on when he fell in the Dog Hole. He wasn't good at this. He was going to make some terrible mistake.

He came to the graveyard, squeezed between two broken slats in the weathered picket fence, and stumbled into a run, dodging stones, leaping graves. Names flashed past, names he knew. The name on the stone nearest the opposite fence stopped him.

Mary Chase: her dates; nothing more.

Phin felt what he always felt here—nothing. Why would her spirit linger? Bittsville was never meant to be their home. She and his father had planned to save their money and buy a shop somewhere; a little shop and a lot of books.

Instead she died in that back room where they'd lived, the eggs and ale and tea sent up by Murray during her brief illness piled uneaten on the table. Unlike in novels, there was no time for a speech. She whispered "Son," or "Sun," and then she stopped; stopped speaking, stopped breathing, though for a long time Phin wasn't sure of that and sat staring at the mysterious movement he was sure he saw in her body—not as large as breathing, more like the shimmer of gases off the culm banks on hot summer afternoons.

Nan Lundy came and said she was dead, closed her eyes, and began doing things. Phin went downstairs, chill and wide-eyed, and that hairy boar Duff Murray poured him a shot of whiskey. It made a thin streak of heat down the middle of him, raw and metallic. He didn't finish it. He saw Murray approve of that.

He should say something now. But "good-bye" felt wrong, and there was no time to think. Phin ducked his head and turned away, over the fence and into the blackberry tunnels.

They led on a long way in leafy darkness, flashes of sunlight, unexpected openings that left him exposed, sudden dead ends. He lost track of how far he'd come, and straightened to look.

Nearly there. He could see the stable roof, below, and a man riding toward town.

He ducked, listening. That was the mule dealer, who'd waited three weeks already for "Little" Bitts, the owner's son, to get back from his Adirondack vacation. What was the man's name? Fraser? Graham? He drank good Scotch, nursing each glass a long time, and rode a horse that was more than good; a dark stallion of extraordinary quality.

Phin risked another look. They'd gone on toward town. The man's back moved easily to the horse's gait. The long coat billowed, and the stallion's flowing tail dusted the ground—off on their daily ride as if nothing out of the ordinary had happened. Phin shuddered and stumbled on through the brambles.

At last the big door yawned before him—the upper level, the hay mow door. Phin watched awhile. When he was sure the barn was empty, he darted across the open space and into its dark shelter.

6
DENNIS

Warm, safe barn smells enveloped Phin—hay, horses, manure. Tears stung his eyes. He sagged against the side of the mow, shaking, seeing Engelbreit fall and fall—

Voices snapped him upright. Out front. Dennis—and someone else. He crept forward and looked through a crack in the wall.

Down in the stable yard, Dennis sat scrubbing a wooden bucket. More buckets were lined up beside him. Pat Mahoney, the Sleeper constable, loomed over him, hands in pockets. His head turned slowly like a suspicious bull's, darting looks into all the corners, while Dennis's acid voice scratched on.

"—kill a man in cold blood and then come in to work! That's just what a murderer'd do. I've a good mind to telegraph Allan Pinkerton about you, Pat; he's always lookin' for detectives! Now get out of here!"

Mahoney took his hands out of his pockets.

"I've got all that boy's work to do, too," Dennis said, "and you've wasted enough of my time. If he shows up, he's finishin' these buckets, I'll tell you that right now! Maybe then I'll think about turning him over."

"Oh, you'll turn him over," Mahoney said.

Dennis splashed more vigorously. Water sloshed on Mahoney's boots. He took a step back, and Dennis stood, tipping his head to meet Mahoney's gaze. Mahoney was a bad man with his fists, a brutal man, but Dennis showed no fear.

"Tryin' to scare me? You'll have to try harder'n that! I got a chunk of cannonball in my leg hurts me every step I take. Had my fill of that, and I've had my fill of fools!"

Mahoney's head lowered; his shoulders bunched. Dennis said, "Your crowd's gone too far; the owners'll smash you like they smashed the union. Oh, you'll have things your own way awhile longer. You can blame that boy and get a jury that'll do what you tell 'em. But you've outsmarted yourselves. I smell it comin'. Your days are numbered!"

Phin's pulse thundered in his ears. Next came the murder.

He'd never be able to stop it. He opened his mouth with that dream-feeling of a shout that wouldn't come. Mahoney cocked his head, as if listening to some deeper meaning within Dennis's words. There was a long pause.

Then Mahoney shoved his hands back in his pockets, glancing around the yard. "You got a good nose, Dennis," he said. "Ain't sayin' you're wrong." Thoughtfully he went out between the gateposts and turned down the Street.

Phin leaned there watching him go. The blood thundered in his temples. The shot hadn't come, no blows even, but his body didn't seem to understand that. He felt flooded with fear and shock. Dennis had taken a risk—

And Dennis, Phin realized suddenly, was standing down in the yard, staring straight up at him.

Phin jerked back, thinking Stop! Stupid.

He was almost stupid enough to come back and look out again. But a second mistake wouldn't put the first one right. He waited, listening. After a moment the splashing resumed.

How could he have been so stupid? His instincts were all wrong for this. Hide. Rest. Maybe his mind would start working again. He crossed to the stairs and eased silently down them.

They brought him to the back row of stalls, empty now. Only the stallion was stabled here, and Phin had just seen him leave. The barn was quiet, dim, and from the old days of hide-and-seek with Jimmy, Phin knew just where to hide. He dropped to his stomach and wormed into the open area under the stairs. It was like a little room, festooned with cobwebs and floored with a deep litter of chaff. Cracks between the stairwell boards gave a view of the corridor and stalls.

Phin hunched there, cradling his arm, staring: at nothing, at the boards, at the cracks between the boards, at the day as it had already happened. Time slowed, blurred. Events happened again in broken flashes, out of sequence. People said their lines over and over.

You're tougher than this, right?

Do you ever sleep, boy?

Tell Ned I said you're to have a penny for your trouble . . . penny for your trouble . . .

Tell Ned—

The wallet. Dangerous. Get rid of it. As long as he had it, he was guilty of a crime. It seemed important not to be guilty.

But it was hard to move. He had to force himself to dig into his pocket and bring out Margaret's package.

The paper had been pounded as he ran and fell and climbed. It was bruised thin, and one corner of the wallet poked through, leather and a fringe of bills.

Phin shuddered. Sometime this evening, down at Murray's, Plume would find out.

A sound in the outer part of the barn came nearer; footsteps, Dennis's distinctive dot-and-carry limp. He turned down the aisle with a bucket and went into the stallion's empty stall. The gray cat followed, taking her own route over the partition and tightrope-walking along it. Phin watched glassily, feeling a hundred miles away.

The cat miaowed at Dennis. He ignored her—worried, or listening. He hung the bucket on its hook, fluffed the stallion's bedding. Bored, the cat jumped down and trotted toward the stairs.

Suddenly she stopped in the middle of the aisle, tail lashing and puffing out till it looked like a raccoon's.

Phin sat rigidly unmoving. The cat growled, a low, throbbing sound that brought Dennis to the stall door. She turned and scuttled toward the other end of the aisle.

"Here, Puss." Dennis reached down and snapped his fingers. She hesitated.

"Now you know there's nothing under there." Dennis spoke in the gentle voice he used only with animals. "Didn't I see Mahoney look? And if your friend was there—well, he'd bide quiet till tonight, wouldn't he? Slip into the wagon when I leave for the station. He's not a complete fool. If he was, they'd have him already."

The cat looked over her shoulder. With another growl she disappeared around the corner. Moving deliberately, as if advertising to the world at large that everything was normal, absolutely normal, Dennis closed the stall door and limped after her.

Phin hugged his knees tight, fighting the urge to run. He wasn't good at this. Found again already; if he didn't get out of here soon, he'd be found by the wrong person, or get some friend in trouble.

But it was broad daylight, and he wasn't a complete fool. Act that way. Think.

He'd do what Dennis said, get to the rail yard, get on a train. How?

Ride the rods; that was one way. There was a cradle of support struts under each car. You could hide there, inches above the rails. Men and boys had traveled the whole country that way—the lucky ones. Fall off, though, and they gathered you up in a basket. Phin shuddered. Not the rods. Not unless he had to.

Thirsty. Hungry, too, in a distant way. He could smell the bacon warming inside his shirt, next to his body—

—Engelbreit's body would be cold by now—

And he had to pee.

No one was near. He could hear Dennis cleaning stalls in another part of the barn. He turned over, dampened the chaff beside him, rolled back to hug his knees. That was the best position. It held him together.

The breaker whistle blew. Boys poured down the Street, running, yelling, fighting. A stickball game began outside. Horses returned from the day's work. Phin heard their measured hoofbeats in the front aisle, snorts, harness shaking. Talk. He couldn't catch much of it; just again and again, "Engelbreit." It startled him every time, brought back the fearless face, turning, falling, the gun leveled next at him—

A quicker set of hooves clopped through the barn. The mule dealer turned the corner, silhouetted in the dim light; hat low over his bearded face, long coat sailing out behind. The stallion followed on a loose rein. A ruddy bar of sunlight slid over shoulder and haunch, revealing the red glow within the apparently black hide.

The stallion sniffed along the floor as he came. Quick and restless, with a tang of wildness in him, he still searched out oats like any ordinary horse. Phin relaxed at the sight, smiling—

As if he heard the smile, the stallion paused, one front foot lifted. For a long moment he stood that way, looking toward the stairwell.

7
Dark Horse

Phin stopped breathing. His heart drummed. He heard the air whistle in the stallion's nostrils, saw them flare, flare, flare.

The mule dealer turned to look at his horse, then glanced briefly toward the stairs. "Aye, lad," he said. "Right enough."

Right enough—the words rang and echoed in Phin's head and he nearly ran—everything in him wanted to, and it took violent effort to stay still. "Can the beast fly?" Mr. Lundy had asked, and the man said, "He can about fly, right enough. . . ."

The oat bin banged open in the other aisle. Dennis was

feeding. The mule dealer led his horse into the stall, and Phin could breathe again. He listened to the sound of unsaddling. Dennis brought oats, exchanged a few words with the mule dealer, clumped up the stairs over Phin's head. Hay shushed down through the trapdoor, and the stallion crunched his supper to the rhythmic swish of brush on silken hide.

Then just eating sounds; nothing human. Phin wouldn't have guessed the man was still in there. Time stretched; the darkness thickened. Phin's mouth was dry, his throat was dry, he was hungry, he ached all over, and it all felt loud, as if hunger and thirst droned inside him, blocked his hearing—

A little sound; creak of leather, flap of a stirrup fender thrown up over the seat. The mule dealer was saddling again. As regular as the breaker whistle for the last three weeks he'd made his appearance at Murray's around now, to eat a sandwich and sip a small whiskey. He never rode there. He always walked.

The stall door opened. The mule dealer came out, closed and latched it, and turned toward the stairs.

Phin sat like a stone. In a moment the boards creaked above him. Dust filtered onto his face. He heard footsteps in the upper story of the barn; then nothing.

Or . . . a rustle? A swish. After several minutes the stallion snorted, a big sound from this horse who usually kept the silence of a wild animal. Saddle leather creaked. "Good lad."

He was in there again. But how?

The only way was the hay hole. He must have dropped through that small trapdoor and landed in the saddle—but why? Who was he?

Lantern light grew and bobbed along the walls. As the mule dealer let himself out of the stall, Dennis came around the corner.

He stopped short. Light swung high as he lifted the lantern. "Something wrong?"

"No, all set."

Dennis took a step closer. "Leavin' his clothes on?"

"Aye, I may go out again shortly."

Dennis grunted. It was a sound that could mean anything. "Thinkin' you'll be in a hurry?"

"I may be in some haste."

The grunt again. "Bridle on, too, eh? Easy to steal him like that. Well, I had a notion to sit out front and smoke a pipe tonight. That'll be a relief to you, won't it—knowin' the door is watched?"

"Aye," the dealer said, and that, too, could mean anything. He walked away down the aisle. Dennis followed, the light receding by jerks. Phin clenched his fists, then splayed his fingers as wide and straight as they would go, a silent scream in the dark. What was going *on*?

A board creaked in the upper floor of the barn. Footsteps paused at the top of the stairs, moved on. From above the stall came a sound of cloth rubbing against wood; then nothing.

Phin strained to hear. Did the man know he was here? What was he? Not a mule dealer, not really. He must be some kind of spy.

A Pinkerton agent? Banks and railroads hired the famous detective agency to catch robbers. Maybe the mine companies had, too.

If this man was a Pinkerton, was that good for Phin, or bad? Would he be viewed as a murderer or a witness?

It didn't matter, he decided, which seat he had in the courtroom. If he was tried, he'd be convicted. If he testified against Plume, he'd be murdered. Dead either way.

The dark thickened and grew velvety. Mice stirred. Cold crept in, and the rich scent of pipe tobacco, good enough to eat. Smells of pork and cabbage drifted from the nearby houses. Phin hugged himself and endured.

After a while, noiselessly, he picked up the package beside him, reached through the worn spot in the paper, and drew out a chunk of folded bills, with a tiny rasping sound like a mouse chewing. He pushed the money deep in his pocket, and left the wallet in the chaff.

Out in the dark a train hooted, like a distant owl. A glow of lamplight warmed the end of the aisle. Dennis must be harnessing the team.

Phin turned on his stomach and oozed, snail-like, from under the stairs. He stood up; new aches and bruises unfolded along his arms, legs, back, reminding him sharply of his fall down the Dog Hole. He stretched up, then down. A joint popped, and the stallion stepped to the stall door.

Shh, Phin thought, heart pounding. He'd been heard—but that tiny pop couldn't reach upstairs, could it?

The door latch rattled, a hoof thumped wood as the stallion reached over the half door. Phin couldn't see him—just a blacker shade of dark—but he knew the head would be reaching, sharp ears pricked, for that extra handful of oats Phin had so often given him.

He crossed the aisle. A velvet muzzle sought his palm, nipping when there were no oats. Sweet, hay-scented breath blew in his ear. Phin shivered.

Good-bye, he mouthed, and went down the dark aisle.

Bang! The stallion kicked the wall. It sounded like a gunshot.

Shocked, Phin blundered into a shovel and sent it clattering. Horses snorted and whinnied and stamped, and Phin ran out the front door into the lantern-lit yard.

The team was only half hitched. Swearing, Dennis fought to fasten the second tug as the gray horse swung wide, shoving, almost trampling him. Phin hesitated, torn between helping and the bushes so invitingly black, the back of the wagon yawning before him, a box, a trap, a hiding hole. . . .

Hooves thundered down the barn aisle. Phin dived up into the wagon, rolled head over heels to the front, and flattened behind a tarp as the stallion galloped out the barn doorway. The rider bent over his neck, long coat billowing out behind. The horse lengthened in a run, up the street toward the depot.

8
TRAIN TO MEET

"Whoa! Now stand—I mean it!"

The horses plunged, making the wagon lurch. Under cover of the noise, Phin drew the tarp over him and lay flat, pressed to the front of the wagon box.

"There now, you old fool—there! What do you think you're going to do, catch him? Now back, back—" A big sigh; Dennis must have fastened the second tug. He kept up a low growl to them as he climbed onto the seat. It sank and squeaked above Phin's head, and the wagon started with a jolt.

"Walk now, walk—all right by jing, *trot* if you're a mind to! What's goin' on around here? Sell up and head west—

got a good mind to! That boy never—And who is *he*? Mule dealer, my eye! Easy, now!"

Should he speak? Phin wondered. An old cuss; that's what Dennis was. He kept his kindness for cats and horses, and a little, unsuspected until today, for Phin. How far would Dennis go for him? Best not to find out; stay quiet, keep the favor nearly accidental—

"*Now* what's he doin'?"

Rub-a-dub rub-a-dub—galloping hooves on the road ahead. Near Phin's face was a rough C-shaped chink of light in the front of the wagon. A knot in the board; heat and sun had shrunk and loosened it. He jabbed it out with his thumb, making a tiny oval window on the lamp-lit street.

Too late. The horseman had passed already—passed and turned and came up beside the wagon.

"Seems I'm going away for a few days," the mule dealer said. "Want to pay my shot in case I don't get back. What do I owe you?"

"I don't carry my figures with me," Dennis said. "You'll have to come to the office."

"No time for that. Here—this should more than cover it."

The wagon checked slightly as the money changed hands; Phin heard the stallion breathing. "Obliged,"

Dennis said in an unobliged voice. "You've waited this long—why don't you stay till morning?"

There was no immediate reply. The stallion danced beside the wagon, a foot away from Phin.

"What do you think about this murder?" the mule dealer asked.

"Don't know much about it."

"The lad worked for you."

"You think Phinny did it?" Dennis asked.

"I don't mind admitting that I have my doubts." The mule dealer's voice was light and nearly laughing. "But I'm a dubious man by nature."

Nearby came the great hoot of the train whistle. "Here she is, right on time," Dennis said, raising his voice. "The Ladybird, bound for Mauch Chunk and points north."

That was for Phin. It wasn't the kind of thing Dennis would say otherwise. Points north. He'd thought of himself as going west, but north would do—

"What's this?" the mule dealer asked.

Now Phin heard voices ahead, and through his knothole saw the shapes of men. They blurred in the wagon's bounce. Five? A dozen? Twenty? The hair prickled on the back of his neck. They'd found him, the lynch mob. They were coming—

The wagon abruptly halted, the body lurching against the pole and rebounding slightly. The group of men steadied in the knothole's frame and there were only three, one to hold each of Dennis's horses, one walking toward the wagon.

The seat screaked as Dennis stood up. "Limpin' Moses, let go of that team, Mahoney, you tin-plate excuse—"

A tall, broad-shouldered shape approached the wagon box. The face came into bright lamplight.

Plume.

Heat flashed on Phin's skin. A cold fist of fear knotted his stomach. Yet he was glad to see Plume. So handsome in the moonlight and lantern light, and hadn't he saved Phin's life? Spared it, anyway. *This one I can't do.*

And there was this. Four people on earth knew— *knew*—that Phin was innocent. One was Ned Plume.

Who said to Dennis, in a dangerous, vibrant voice, "Where is the little rat?"

"If you mean Phinny—"

"You know who I mean."

"I ain't seen him."

"I want him," Plume said, ignoring the radiant honesty of Dennis's voice. "He's taken something from me."

"A murderer *and* a thief," Dennis said. "Boy's had a big day!"

Plume's eyes seemed to flare. He went very still. "I'll take no lip from you, Dennis. He has my pocketbook, and he's taken something else besides."

"No man likes to be parted from his money," Dennis said, voice bristling like the back of an angry dog. "You least of all, I hear."

Plume said, "That wallet's worth the lives of six men."

Mahoney's head jerked in surprise. That shouldn't have been said, except in a low voice at one of Murray's back tables. Plume's eyes glittered with drink and fathomless rage; a dangerous man, loosed from self-restraint, yet master of his body, swift to act and react. His friends would be careful in their speech, down at Murray's. Phin would bring the next drink quickly, and quickly efface himself.

But Dennis wouldn't heed these signals. He was fearless himself by long habit, like a terrier or a bantam rooster. He'd say something dangerous; there was nothing he could say that wasn't dangerous. Phin drew his legs under him, ready to hurl himself over the side and run. Draw them off Dennis—he could do that, anyway. Maybe he'd even get away—

"Why would the lad still be around?" The mule dealer; mild, friendly sounding. "If he murdered a man, he'd be on the run, wouldn't he? And if he's got your wallet,

Plume, he's got the wherewithal to run a long way."

Plume's body relaxed slightly. "That he does."

"What else has he taken?" Yes. Phin wanted to know that too, as he lay with legs half bent, between run and stay.

"That's no man's business but my own," Plume said in a cold, level voice. At the horses' heads, Mahoney yawned like a nervous dog.

"Well, you gents settle in and enjoy your little chat," Dennis said. "I've got freight to haul and a bed I'd like to climb into before sunup."

Plume turned his head toward the station. "That's the Ladybird, isn't it? People I should talk to up line." He sprang onto the seat beside Dennis. "Mahoney, hop on! When we get there, hold her a minute. A couple of messages I'll need to be sending. Mac, you too."

Behind Phin, boots rapped on the bare wood floor of the wagon. Dennis said something angry. Footsteps came toward Phin. A boot crunched down on his shin, slid off it, drew back and kicked his leg out of the way like a piece of firewood.

A muttered conversation ensued. Phin heard none of it. His shin felt on fire, as if it must be dripping blood. Sick, dazed, he lay against the wagon front, clenching his teeth, struggling not to groan.

The wagon stopped. He heard the mighty *shh* and *sss* of the steam locomotive. The wagon jounced as Mahoney jumped off and ran to catch the engineer. In a moment Plume and the other man were gone. Rap of boots on the platform; light prance and champ of the stallion moving on somewhere.

Phin flexed his leg. It moved. Hurt; hurt worse than his arm this morning, even, but it moved.

"Your freight's in, Dennis," a new voice said. "Half ton of sacked western oats—"

"I'll just swing around," Dennis said, and started the wagon again with a jerk. Phin felt it make a wide arc away from the platform. He put his eye to the knothole. Coal cars were being pushed up the track to make the end of this mixed train. A passenger car. A plump man in a long coat walked the platform. Plume and the man Mac stood with their heads close together, Mac listening hard.

"Whoa," Dennis said, and went on conversationally. "Phinny, if you're there—freight car half open behind you, and you won't find a better chance. Grab that sack in the corner. If you ain't there, I'm a fool like everybody else in this forsaken hole—but I ain't lookin', so I won't know. Now go!"

Phin groped in the corner with one cold hand, found what felt like a flour sack. He siezed it, thrust back the tarp, and leaped low over the side of the wagon. His leg would either hold him or it wouldn't. He'd find out when he landed.

9
HOLD OR FOLD

He hit the ground awkwardly and stumbled upright, not sure, for a moment, if he could take another step. His leg had a decision to make; fold, because his shinbone seemed to be breaking in half, or hold.

It held. Hurt, and held. He hobbled to the black opening. The floor of the car was chest high and smooth, and his first try at getting in amounted to a feeble hop.

"Hey Dennis," a voice called. "Move it, will you? They need to pull up—"

He'd lose his cover. Phin threw the flour sack into the car and scrambled after it, hooking his elbow on the edge of the door to haul himself up. His hurt shin scraped across the lip of the doorway; small bright pain-lights flared in his head.

He rose to his feet. The bundle had loosened inside his shirt, and biscuit crumbs rolled down his ribs. In front of him his own shadow loomed up the back wall, a crippled giant. He scooped up the sack, dodged into the pitch black beyond the light, and banged into another wall; stacked crates, filling half the car.

With a sigh and rumble the train began to creep toward the platform, toward Mac and Mahoney and Plume.

Phin felt frantically up the crate cliff. Above his head he found the top. He threw his sack up; it fell back on him; he threw it harder and higher and climbed after it, finding tiny finger- and toeholds in the sides of crates and boxes. The train lurched gently as he flung himself over the top, groping for his sack.

It was nowhere in reach. He rose on his knees and bumped his head on the ceiling. Crawl, then. Reach, crawl—

His right hand came down on nothing, and his arm plunged up to the shoulder into nothing.

He drew back with a gasp. A hole between crates—he felt around its edges. It was narrow, not like the Dog Hole. He couldn't have fallen in. But with a whole railcar to choose from, the flour sack had. It had been knobby, and landed with a promising thump. There must have been food in it; lost.

The train stopped with a deep metallic squeal. Yellow lamplight came in the door now, and Phin heard voices. This car was at the platform, and he was up here with no place to hide. The boxes were packed level, a broad, flat plane stretching toward the door.

Voices, louder, closer; Phin curled in the back corner, pulled his cap down, and turned his face to the wall. He and Jimmy had learned by the age of five—hide your face, hide your eyes. It's the eyes that give you away.

Hoofbeats again. He'd been haunted all day by the horse and Engelbreit. The horse, at least, he'd soon leave behind—

"Never heard of such a thing!" said an unknown voice.

"I find that hard to believe." The mule dealer, just outside the door. "Surely from time to time a man needs to transport a horse."

"Then they wait for a stock car!" The speaker sounded peppery.

"As it happens, it's this very now that I need to travel, and on this very car that I'll go. Unless you'd rather explain to the gentleman who signed this pass—"

"This railroad gives no free passes!"

"Then that's not his signature?"

A seething silence. The horse snorted and stamped. Free pass, Phin thought. So this man worked for the mine owners. They and the railroad owners were the same class, sometimes the same people. The mule dealer, as he styled himself, must be a Coal and Iron policeman, or a Pinkerton agent.

"Oh, very well—Bill, Jamie, bustle! This gentleman needs a ramp and bait for the horse, and a bucket, and—I don't know what all, but get it and hurry! We're holding trains all up and down the line!"

A moment later the door rumbled wider.

Phin waited numbly. In a moment they'd discover him. It all had been for nothing—

A thump. Footsteps on the bare floor. Hay rustled, and a man said, "Oh, it's blowin' right out his ears, the steam! Ye can fair see it!"

Holding his cap low over his face, Phin risked a glance toward the light. The men were close, but he couldn't see them. He was too high, too far back. Below the wall of crates they were only voices.

If he couldn't see them, they couldn't see him.

And that meant—there was a heavier-sounding thump

as they laid a ramp up to the open door—that meant that he wasn't discovered after all. Not yet.

A nervous pair of pointed ears appeared in the doorway. Shod hooves rang on the floor, and the mule dealer's voice, dark as black coffee, spoke reassurance. "Easy, lad. That's the way—leave the ramp. I'll want to get him in and out. No, he won't need tying. I'll ride with him."

No, Phin thought. No.

He pressed into the corner, clawed his fingers into the smooth angle of the walls. There was no gap. This enormous seamless box had just one opening, now guarded by the mysterious man who had followed him all day.

The walls squeezed him. His pulse drummed in his ears, a tiny sound, a dense sound, on and on and—

"Fraser?"

At the car door, incredulous; Plume again. "What are you doing?"

"Taking the cars north, Plume. Like yourself."

"Odd way to do it, all of a sudden." Plume's voice was cold with suspicion.

"Maybe I killed that man this morning," Fraser said. "Maybe I'm on the run."

"Then you're drawing a lot of attention to yourself."

"Reckless, could be. Fool, could be. Or could be I'm a

man who'll do what he takes a notion to, and doesn't care to be questioned. However,"—Fraser's tone, which had become dangerous, lightened—"they're wanting to move their train, and here's you and me holding them up. Will you ride a ways with me? Pleasant pile of hay here, and an extremely pleasant flask."

"I have a flask my own self," Plume said.

"Two's company."

Deep in his cocoon of torment, Phin waited for the second refusal. It had to come. Plume must walk away. He must. . . .

"Well then, I will," Plume said, with sudden, entirely unbelievable friendliness. He shouted to someone far off: "Ridin' in with Fraser and the horse. My ticket's punched!"

No, Phin thought. No—

There was a scritch of gravel, an impact, a grunt, as Plume pulled himself into the car. Phin's skin prickled, hairs rising all down his back. Sweat broke on his forehead. Like his leg, his spirit had a decision to make.

He laughed—weakly, just one helpless, nearly silent breath, and sagged in the corner, shaking his head, as Dennis's voice echoed in his mind.

All right, then. Come on in if you're a mind to!

10
LINING OUT

The whistle wailed. Chuffing, the train gained momentum.

"Down," Fraser said at the bottom of the crate wall. "Aye, I mean it! Down." A thud, a horse-sized grunt. "Good lad!"

"Like a dog!" Plume said. "He laid down for you just like a dog!"

Really? In the three weeks the horse had stayed at Dennis's, Phin had never caught him sleeping. He was too alert. He'd be on his feet, shaking straw off his sleek sides, before anyone could get near. It would be worth seeing a horse like that folded up on a boxcar floor.

But Phin wasn't tempted to look. He leaned back in the corner, speed dragging at him as the train lined out across the dark land.

The sides of the car shook, the crates shook, faster and faster until the shakes smoothed to a steady vibration. The wheels clacked. Through the partly open door, moon shadows leaped on the walls. The train plunged on. *Faster and faster*, it said, in a hundred clacking, creaking, rattling voices. *Faster and faster, fasterandfaster.*

And louder. Phin hadn't imagined it would be like this—the clacking, the whistle's blare, the walls shuddering fit to shake their rivets out. A moving train was a forest of sound.

Sheltered within it, he stretched his legs. Probably it made a noise. Probably the cloth of his pants hissed or rasped. Probably his boot heels thumped on the crates. It didn't matter. Not even he could hear it.

He passed a hand down his shinbone. There was an enormous goose-egg swelling, like the one on his arm. He'd had hurts like these before and thought nothing of them. These injuries came in life-and-death struggle and seemed more important, but really they were just bruises—

No. Don't think of that—Engelbreit's head hitting the

stove. He was safe for the moment; he must stop frightening himself.

He reached inside his shirt for his bundle. Bacon fat had soaked through the bandanna. He felt a slick of it on his skin. The biscuits were crumbly. He stuffed one in his mouth; salty and smoke flavored from its daylong association with the meat, better than anything he'd ever eaten.

Dry, though. He'd last had water when? Jimmy's bottle, at the lip of the Dog Hole, a long time ago.

"Nay," Fraser said below, and went on. To make out his words, Phin had to do the special thing with his ears that he'd learned at Murray's. It was a kind of relaxing, not fighting the unwanted sounds, but letting them pass like water—water again!—through a sieve, catching only what he wanted. Up here he did what he couldn't at Murray's, cupped a hand behind his ear and pointed it at Fraser the way a horse would.

He netted Fraser mid-sentence. "—won't be buyin' mules just now, I'm thinkin'. They'll wait till things quiet down. But there's an outfit up north may be interested."

"What outfit?"

"That'd be telling."

"So tell," Plume said.

At Murray's his voice would make a little silence around

it. From across the room Murray would catch Phin's eye, jerk his head toward the back door. Phin would drift that way and be out of the room before anything started. He'd heard many fights at Murray's, but rarely seen one.

Fraser broke the dangerous pause. "I'm like you," he said. "Not answerable to myself alone. The man I work for wouldn't want me telling his business to all and sundry."

It was the equivalent of saying, *I know you're a Sleeper.* Not wise, not wise at all. Everyone could know these things as long as everyone pretended not to. Fraser should know that. He'd only spent three weeks in Bittsville, but he was no stranger to coal country ways.

"Drink?" Fraser asked.

"Got my own," Plume said. "Thanks anyway!" The forced lightness in his voice made the hairs rise on the back of Phin's neck. Plume was suspicious. He wanted to know more before he did something irreversible. "Fine horse," he said. "If your mules are anything to compare—"

"They are, as mules go."

"Don't speak ill of mules. There's some down there could run the mine themselves."

"Too smart," Fraser said. "Smarter than horses. They won't work themselves to death like a horse will. Always wondered why they'll go into a mine at all."

"We go," Plume said. "It's not so bad."

"I'd rather slave in a cotton field under the sky and a whip than go down in a mine. Not *bad*?"

"We're tougher than you Scots, aren't we? Make the world go. It's us down there with black powder and picks movin' this train right now. The world rides on the backs of Irishmen."

The open doorway dimmed as if they'd passed into a wood. Fraser said, "More than just Irish. There's all kinds of folk bent down with toil. English, even."

"English?" Plume's voice was cold and vibrant. "You take your share of risks, mule man."

Were weapons drawn? If they fought, someone would die. There was no escape in this moving box, no chance to miss.

But Fraser, like a man who pulls a cat's tail, then strokes her when she scratches, said, "Nay, I meant nothing by it. I'm all for peace. War makes a man want peace and quiet, don't you agree?"

"How'd you know I fought in the war?"

Fraser sighed theatrically. "A guess. Just a guess. Come, man, lay your hackle! I only want someone to talk to. The horse is a braw lad, but he's no much for conversation!"

"Fair enough," Plume said shortly. "What d'you say to a game of cards? Is there light enough?"

Apparently there was. Their voices dropped, and Phin could no longer make out the words. He moved his tongue in his dry mouth to work up a little spit. Water would be good.

They'd poured water for the stallion. He remembered the crash of it coming at him through that haze of insanity. It was down there now, dark surface shivering with the movement of the train. Black, with silver moonlit ripples. The stallion, whenever he wanted, could dip his muzzle in and flood the thirsty crevices of his mouth. Coolly it would glide down his throat—

Stop thinking about water.

He took the bundle on his lap and turned its contents over. Three biscuits left, and a lot of crumbs. He licked his finger, dampening it, and pushed it onto them to pick them up, cleaning out the whole bandanna that way. The bacon taste was strong and there was some other taste, too, wild yet mellow. At first he thought it was the wood of the matchbox. He put the box in his pocket so it wouldn't get greasy, felt for more crumbs, counted his biscuits again—three, and one so small it was hardly worth saving.

He picked it up and suddenly knew this wasn't a biscuit. He sniffed; tears started in his eyes.

It was a plug of tobacco—the cheap kind that breaker boys chewed, and mule boys. He'd seen everything Mrs. Lundy put into this bundle, could see in his mind's eye each motion of her hands. This had been slipped in later. Only Jimmy could have done that.

When Jimmy'd gone into the breaker, he'd started chewing. All the boys did. Tobacco juice kept you from coughing, made the juices flow. Man enough to work, man enough to chew—that was the idea.

Phin had tried it. It made him puke. It made everyone puke until they got the hang of it, but Phin quit and Jimmy kept on, and that was the difference between Phin Chase and Jimmy Lundy. Jimmy, in Phin's place, would—

Would what? Phin opened his eyes. What could Jimmy do that he wasn't doing? Traveling with his enemy like this, even Jimmy Lundy would lay low, wait his chance to get away.

So he was doing all right, maybe. He turned the tobacco in his fingers.

Makes the juices flow.

He licked it, gingerly. Springs and fountains opened in the back of his mouth and he nearly gagged. He swallowed, swallowed again—

"Slowing down?" Fraser. The voices were suddenly clearer.

"We're never there yet!" Plume said. The train came to a slow, sighing stop. The quiet was astonishing. Then she began to creep backward.

"Ah," Fraser said. "They're pulling onto a spur to let another train pass. Aye, lad, get up!"

The stallion's hooves scraped and thudded on the floor. Then Phin heard Fraser walking him in a circle, giving him the chance to stretch his legs. To Plume he said, "So they took you off to fight, you were saying, and you just a lad?"

"Made a man of me!" Plume sounded bitter.

Fraser said, "I don't know what it made of me."

"Conscripted?"

"Volunteered." Fraser laughed shortly. "Hard to imagine when you've got to the other end of it, but there's no fathoming the notions in a boy's head. So I'm only a little surprised at that murder back there. I know what boys are capable of."

"When I get through with him," Plume said, "that boy won't be capable of anything."

Every atom in Phin's body went still.

"Saw him around the stable," Fraser said after a pause.

"Quiet, good with the horses—well, this one liked him, and he doesn't take to many." The horse had stopped moving; he started it walking again. "And yet he killed a man—do you believe that?"

Phin heard the sound of Plume's deep-drawn breath. "Engelbreit drove men he shouldn't drive and fired men he shouldn't fire."

"This lad won't have killed him for that," Fraser said. "He was never—"

Plume interrupted him, in a voice that shook with fury. "I don't make war on kids. She knows that. I meant for him to run. But when I catch him now, kid or no kid—I'll cut his throat."

11
WATER

The approaching train shrieked. The horse dropped manure, and Fraser said, "Step away from the door and I'll kick these out. We'll have a pleasanter ride."

There were scuffing sounds. Fraser went on. "You'll not be content to just take back your property, then? Or turn the boy over to the law?"

"No." Plume's voice steadied, vibrant with anger. "If I'm the kind of man she says, I'll *be* that man. Double that man. I've held myself to a standard—well, what good did that do me when she won't even—"

The other train shrieked again, passing close, buffeting their car with wind and drowning Plume's words. But

Phin didn't need to hear more. He could see the scene, the smoke and lamplight and Margaret on her stool nursing that slow first whiskey. Did they tell of the killing first, brag of their strange mercy, not killing but framing him, letting him run? Or did Margaret start it, asking if Plume had gotten his wallet, she gave it to Phin Chase to leave here?

However it started, it ended with the eagles tearing at each other. Margaret must have flown out bitterly at Plume in front of everyone. She might not care about Engelbreit, but she was fond of Phin and she'd loved his mother, and that was the end of Ned Plume.

The train passed in a last gust of wind and noise. In the sudden quiet Fraser said, "So the wallet's the least of it, even with that in it."

"What's your meaning, mule man?" Plume's voice was like steel. "What should a wallet have in it besides money?"

"Six men's lives. You said yourself—"

"What surprises me about you," Plume said, "—and I don't like surprises, mind!—is how you keep asking questions. Most people in coal country learn it's not healthy."

Fraser hadn't asked a question, Phin was almost sure. He'd only said things, provocative things, like a man slipping a ferret down a rat hole to see what would come out.

Plume said, "Let's talk mules. Where's your jack stock from? What you got for mares?"

"The jacks are out of Maryland—I'd rather have Kentucky, but you know how it is. The mares, though—"

Fraser went on about his mules, making them sound like the best mules ever to set foot in a mine, just as a real salesman would. But were there any mules? Phin doubted it.

He touched the roll in his pocket. Worth the lives of six men? But all he had was money, right?

The train began to move. Soon it was plunging cross-country behind its own self-important shout—*Out of my way! Out of my way.*

The men grew quieter. Miles passed—miles of sketching escape plans that would have worked perfectly, if only Phin didn't need a clear path to the door; miles of licking the tobacco, trying to pretend that quenched a thirst; miles of dozing, half dreaming, negotiating the quicksand complexities of coal country only to jerk awake to the sound of a gunshot, and remember.

Finally the whistle blew, the brakes made their long silvery squeal, and the train came to a stop.

A station; yellow lantern light made the shadows blacker. Irish voices called back and forth. Something thumped on the roof above Phin's head, and footsteps walked along the top of the car, then jumped to the next one. The horse snorted and scrambled up. "Shh," Fraser said. "It's only noise."

Outside the car door someone said, "Plume? Ned Plume?" Phin recognized the voice. Occasionally men from high in the organization visited Murray's, men who cast silence before them like other men cast a shadow. Phin couldn't put a face to this voice, but he'd heard it; heard, and been motioned out of the room by a jerk of Murray's head.

Plume answered carelessly. "Yeah. Here." He jumped down from the boxcar, and his voice was lost in station bustle.

"How long are we stopping?" Fraser asked someone outside.

"Five minutes, ten at the most."

"I need fresh water for the horse. Here." Probably he handed the man a bill. Phin touched the money in his pocket. Money could pave the way—if only he could get out!

The stallion seemed to feel the same. His hooves rang and banged on the bare wood floor, and Fraser kept turning him from the door.

The man returned. Water crashed into the tub. Fraser

said, "They're looking for a boy, right? Overhead?"

"Overhead, under the cars—they'd have looked in this hay, only Plume himself was riding on it. Kid went south, likely, or he came through on an early freight."

"What's he look like?"

You *know* what I look like! Phin thought.

"What does any boy look like? Dark hair, I think they said. Doesn't have a coat, unless he stole one somewhere."

"Can't ride the rods if he doesn't have a coat."

"Not for long!" the man said cheerfully. "Freeze and fall off and be cut to mincemeat. Likely that's what happened to him."

"Aye, right enough."

Voices outside. The whistle blew, and a giant shadow loomed on the back wall.

"Thought you were stopping here," Fraser said. He sounded slightly disconcerted.

"I'm not." Plume's voice was darker, flatter.

"I've enjoyed your company," Fraser said. "Don't think I haven't. But wouldn't you be more comfortable in the passenger car?"

The train had begun to move. Plume shouted out the door at someone. "You catch him, he's mine! Spread the word. Not Mahoney's or anybody else's. Mine."

Now his voice was inside again. "I'm ridin' here. I don't feel like talk, and I do feel like drink."

After a moment Fraser said, "No talk, then. But—a bite to eat? You'll want to lay a foundation—no? Fair enough!"

The next leg of the journey was longer and thirstier. Phin couldn't make himself eat another biscuit, not without a drink first. His mouth produced less saliva all the time, and the tobacco gave less relief. In the breaker the boys had water bottles. They could snatch a swallow from time to time, at the risk of missing a piece of slate and getting a beating.

Envying the breaker boys; would his mother laugh? She could laugh at bitter things, even as she rolled up her sleeves to do something about them. She'd smile, at least, at it turning out that Phin would have been safer if he'd defied her. Though it wasn't safety she'd wanted for him so much as a way out, and he was going.

Oh, but a drink, though. He lay through the night in the endlessly rocking railcar, half dreaming of her washtub and the slosh of soapy water.

It was nearly dawn when they stopped next. The square of light on the wall was pearly gray and there was a smell of dew and grass. Half awake, Phin heard Plume ask,

"Where's this?" Unsteady, abrupt; he must have been drinking all night. Someone answered—a word Phin didn't hear—and Plume jumped out, falling, swearing.

Fraser asked how long the stop was. "Twenty minutes," was the answer, and he bought someone's assistance in laying the ramp.

Phin listened to it thud into place. His tongue was thick and cottony, and so was his head. The back of his throat hurt. When he swallowed, it felt like it was going to break open, like a half-healed wound.

Saddle leather creaked. The stallion's hooves rang on the wood floor, the sound diminishing down the ramp. Some distance away Fraser said, "All right then, lad." Next came the tremendous gush of the stallion urinating.

Phin sat up. Where were they?

The stallion *clip-clopped* away toward the front of the train. Plume was—where? There were voices, but not close.

This was his chance.

He rose on hands and feet and scrambled across the crates, let himself down over the edge, groping for fingerholds and toeholds. An overhead searcher thumped onto the car and walked along it. Phin must be very quick, very good, as he had planned—drop and crawl under the car, and come out the other side running.

His toes touched the floor. He eased down soundlessly and turned.

In the back corner stood a wooden tub, a third full of water.

Phin didn't think. He was past thinking. He crossed the car in two long steps, dropped to his knees, and plunged his face in.

Beautiful, the wet, the cool. He sucked it in. Bits of hay floated against his lips. He smelled horse and wet spicy oak wood and he drank it down and down, rested, and drank again.

Enough. That's what he'd have told a thirsty horse. Stop, or you'll get sick. He glanced toward the door. The rail yard was a wide expanse of gravel seamed with track. Once Phin was out there, he'd be exposed. Good thing it was still so dark.

A bottle lay on the floor, gleaming in the pale light.

A bottle. He could fill it.

It was very near the door, and as he took a cautious step toward it Phin discovered he was afraid; afraid of the light, gray and grainy as it was. Afraid of the open space, and the voices, and the hoofbeats.

He made himself dart forward anyway and snatch the bottle up. No cork; he couldn't hunt for it, and some of the water would slosh out, but most would stay in, for a while anyway. He pushed the bottle under the surface and jumped at the glugging sound it made. Hurry, hurry. He pulled it out, dripping, before it was full, and turned.

Plume was coming.

For an endless moment Phin stood frozen as Plume crossed the tracks, head down, watching his feet. His miner's cap was pulled low over his eyes.

He tripped. Phin dived for the shadows, closed his teeth around the top of the bottle, and scrambled up the crate wall. Water sloshed into his mouth, nearly choking him. Up and over and back, light on hands and feet, and into his corner. Plume got back in, then Fraser and the stallion, and the now-familiar departure noises began.

He'd missed his chance.

Well, he had water now, and if they were searching this train on Ned Plume's orders, then he wasn't out of coal country yet. Maybe it was all for the best. Phin took a sip of the whiskey-tainted water. A drop went down the wrong pipe and he coughed.

Just once. He stifled the next in the crook of his elbow. Tears streamed down his face, his nose ran, his ribs heaved spasmodically, but he held the coughs inside him.

"Aye," Fraser said soothingly. "Walk a bit more, lad, if

that's how you feel." Hooves banged on the floor, providentially making a cover of sound. Phin let out one more cough—he had to or burst—and the train began to wheeze and whisper, hiding his own wheezes. He sat up, weak and wet faced, and saw a small clothy hump on top of the crate a few feet away.

The sack. Dennis's sack. It hadn't fallen in the hole after all. When the train sounds had risen to a safe level, Phin crawled over on his stomach, drew it back to his corner, and opened it.

Apples, bruised and cornery, with a lovely scent rising from them. A chunk of the good brown bread the boardinghouse cook made. At the bottom, a small Barlow knife. Its blade was worn almost to a sickle shape; Dennis used it for everything from harness repairs to carving off chunks of tobacco to paring hooves.

Phin's eyes smarted. He stretched them wide.

Well.

Well.

He had a knife now. What a man needed—a knife to cut his tobacco with.

12
OUT

Sunrise struck wavering red rays through the partly open door. The back wall of the car flashed bright and honey colored, rippling with the shadows of trees they passed. Sheltered in train noise, Phin stretched, peed down a crack behind the crates, ate an apple, all in spacious golden daylight.

There were two stops that morning. Both times Plume got out, once Fraser and the horse did, but Phin never saw another chance to escape unseen.

At the third stop the searchers hauled someone to Plume near the car, someone who spoke quick and stammering in a language Phin had never heard.

"Does that look like a boy?" Plume hit the man—at least, somebody hit somebody. Phin heard the smack and a grunt from Fraser, who must be watching out the open door. A few minutes later Plume got back in and a cork popped.

After this they traveled a long time without stopping. The car heated. Dark drips appeared on the ceiling. Phin touched one, and his fingers came away sticky with tar. He heard the sound of splashing a couple of times—Fraser putting water on the horse to cool him.

That would feel good, but Phin didn't have water to waste. Not enough to last the day, truth be told.

He ate another apple and his last biscuit; recited poetry under his breath, reaching back to the distant past— yesterday morning—when he'd been himself, when his life was recognizable. Train rhythm became washboard rhythm, and he could imagine his mother was there. But not for long.

At last he took out the roll of money.

His hands jumped when he saw the printed numbers. He'd never held one bill of this size, let alone—he rifled through them—four, five, six, se—no, that was a folded piece of paper.

Did he have it, then? He'd been sure that whatever it

was had been left under Dennis's stairs. He started to unfold it.

His hands shook.

That stopped him. He sat for a while staring at the folded sheet. The letters might as well be Chinese— upside down, backward, bleeding through the cheap paper. What could it be? A letter? Orders? Worth the lives of six men—Sleepers? Intended victims? Maybe also the life of one boy, if he made the right bargain.

In which case he should read it.

Or he shouldn't.

He already knew more about the Sleepers than most people, growing up at Murray's. But what he knew was put together from shreds that wouldn't seem like evidence to anyone else. Shreds were safe. Shreds could be denied. This—

He folded the bills around the paper, stuffed the roll into his pocket. Think about this. He already knew one thing he couldn't forget. Maybe he'd better keep it that way.

The paper made him think of Margaret. After his mother's death she'd taken him on, watched over him in her way. It used to embarrass Phin, being singled out by her with men like Plume watching. She'd known that. It amused her. She's no fool, his mother used to say, and now he wondered: had her attention saved his life? Was that why Plume hadn't shot him?

Saved him only to doom him twenty minutes later.

Plume spoke abruptly; Phin adjusted his ears to catch him mid-sentence: "—unnerstand is killin'."

His voice was slurred and struggling; a man at the head-on-table stage, driven to tell all he knew before oblivion took hold. "All through the strike—'don' do nothin', no violence,' they said. An' we held our fire. An' what happened? They broke the union, an' now we've . . . got . . . nothin'."

Phin touched the money in his pocket. Not exactly. But many did have nothing. All summer families had scoured the woods for mushrooms and berries, leaving the land bare and beaten seeming. After that, the sound of the breaker had meant defeat, but also life.

"You're working again," Fraser said.

"Twenty-six percent pay cut! An' they're closin' shafts. Every—every job they cut . . . b'longs to an Irish. Tell me that's right. Tell a kid he can't eat tonight 'cause Pop came from . . . from Ireland. He don't care! He's a kid; he's here. Wants to eat. So what are you going to do? Let it keep on like that?"

"No," Fraser said after a bit. "Got to fight, I guess. But who? It's not just one man—it's a kingdom."

"Machine," Plume said. "Put in an Irishman, turn the crank. Out drops a dollar. So who—who d'you fight? You fight—everybody. Fight the whole—whole place. Startin' . . . with . . . that kid."

"He's just a kid," Fraser said. "He's here."

Phin's heart skipped in his throat. He drew his legs under him, ready to dive out the door—

"Wants to eat," Fraser went on, and Phin realized he was quoting Plume's words back to him, pulling the cat's tail again. Next would come the quarrel, then the soothing.

But there was no response. After a while Fraser said, "Sweet dreams, pal! And now what?"

There was a restless note in his voice. The stallion got up with a thump and scrape. "Nay then," Fraser said. "Let's think a bit."

Phin leaned back in his corner. He felt more uneasy with Plume unconscious than he had with both enemies wide awake. Plume and Fraser had canceled each other out. Now there was only Fraser—whoever he was. Whatever he wanted.

Get off now, the train seemed to say. Get off now

getoffnowgetoffnow. Phin sat rubbing his leg muscles back to life, listening for the sounds that Fraser persistently did not make.

A long time later the train stopped again.

The stallion rose, impatient, quick moving. "Nay, don't step on him." There was a dragging sound. "Now, what am I going to do with you?" Fraser said. "What am I going to do at all?"

Get out, Phin thought. Because I am! He rose, half crouching under the low ceiling, and tucked the flour sack into his belt. Without a cork the bottle wasn't worth taking, but the sack would come in handy.

With the train still, the sound cover was gone. Phin only moved when the stallion did. Fortunately the animal was as restless as he was. Soon Phin was far enough forward to see Fraser at the open door, staring at—

What? Phin could see nothing but green and shadows. He had the impression of late afternoon, smelled apples and fresh pine sawdust. A breeze whirled the hay chaff into the air and the sun caught it, turning it to shifting golden needles.

Fraser sighed.

There was a second sigh, and Phin realized with a

terrible start that the stallion had raised his head. The brilliant dark eyes were fixed on him.

The stallion lifted his head minutely, lowered it, lifted again, as if sampling separate layers of air current. His nostrils flared, red as glowing coals. The sharp-cut ears focused on Phin for a long moment. Then one slanted at the man in the doorway.

Phin almost put a finger to his lips. Don't, he mouthed, knowing that was ridiculous. He was mesmerized by the movement in the delicate skin above the nostrils. It seemed to purl like flowing water or like smoke. He knew he should sink back out of sight, but he couldn't, didn't, until he heard footsteps outside. Then he crouched, turning his face away.

"What's all this?" someone said at the door. "Why are you riding here?"

Fraser said, "It's all right."

"All right? This car's supposed to be half empty. There's supposed to be room for a shipment of furniture." The man wasn't noticeably Irish; Phin wondered where they were.

"It's all right," Fraser repeated. "I have this."

"What about him?" the voice said a moment later, grudgingly.

"He's traveling with me," Fraser said. "Know who this is? You're lookin' at Ned Plume."

"Never heard of him."

"A lot of people have. If you know what I mean."

"I don't," the man outside said firmly. "Never been mixed up in any of that."

"Whatever it is," said a second voice. Phin hadn't realized there were two of them.

"Don't be a fool!" the first man snapped. He crunched away.

"This'll be a long wait," the second man said. "She'll be taking on water when we're cleared to pull in."

"How long?"

"An hour. Maybe two."

Fraser said, "Then we'll get out for a bit."

"Too steep for the ramp, I'm thinkin'."

"He'll jump."

"And back in? I'll admire to see that. He's a fine Morgan."

"No." Fraser sounded occupied; saddling, likely. "Caught him wild on the northern plains—"

"That's a Morgan," the trainman said flatly. "Stood the trip well, hasn't he? Just a little nervous-like. Now what about him?"

The saddlebags slapped into place. "Sick," Fraser said. "Contracted it from the neck of a bottle! Is there a doctor in town?"

"There is—white house next to the store. Got a little of the same sickness, from what I hear."

"Then maybe he knows the cure. I'll ride up and see if he'll take my friend in charge." Leather creaked as Fraser mounted.

Phin curled tight, arms around his knees. His heart beat so loudly he thought Fraser must hear it. Why hadn't he waited? Just a few minutes, and he would have been able to leave safely, but he'd been impatient and now Fraser's head was level with the stallion's. All he had to do was turn his head—

"Stand back!" Fraser said. There was a scraping sound, the crunch of gravel, then a sudden sense of air and empti-ness in the car and a drumbeat of hooves outside, rapidly receding. The trainman whistled. "Look at him go!"

Then the voice spoke through the open door: "In a bad way, ain't you? Wouldn't want to have your head right now!"

Phin hunched, holding his breath, until the man walked away. Then he scrambled across the crates.

Plume was down there. Phin could see his boots pointing slackly toward the ceiling. But there'd been no sound from him. Passed out, Phin hoped. Anyway there was no choice. He let himself rapidly down.

Plume lay boneless against a pillow of hay, his face pale and slick with sweat. He seemed unable to move, but his eyes followed Phin, dark, narrow, and filled with hate.

13
PURSUIT

He'd never been hated before. He was never important enough to hate. The look almost stopped him; but then Plume tried to move and Phin was out the door.

Bright, so bright. Blinking, he made out a fat man in overalls stumped away up track. Beyond him the world blurred red, scarlet, and orange—trees in their fall colors. A distant gray steeple floated above them, transparent against the blue sky.

Plume groaned and scuffed the floor, trying to get up; Phin ducked between cars to the other side of the train, where a green meadow sloped up to a bright wood. He jumped down the railroad grade and ran.

It felt effortless. His long afternoon shadow raced ahead of him up the grass. Insects leaped wildly out of his way. A crow squawked and angled off into the sky.

But the steep hill quickly sapped his strength. He stumbled in an unseen swale and almost fell. Watch out! Holes.

No, this wasn't coal country. Was it? Chest heaving, he turned to look back.

A landscape of fields, farms, stone walls spread before him. Patches of colorful woodland were thrown over the knees of the hills like quilts. No breaker buildings loomed. No scars of digging or heaps of mine waste marred the earth. The train was the only industrial thing in sight, tended by little figures of men up near the engine. A lady's bonnet poked out a window of the passenger car like a daisy.

Phin walked on. His legs felt weak, his head throbbed, train noise echoed in his skull—but he was someplace else, someplace new. Birds. Treetops sighing in the wind. Whisper of falling leaves.

No tavern talk. No breaker. No explosions underground. The air was fresh and spicy, like the stray breeze that morning at Engelbreit's.

He stepped into the shadow of the woods and turned to look back. A tiny horse and rider and a miniature buggy came from the direction of the steeple. Fraser'd found his doctor.

Would Plume mention having seen him? Would he even remember? He was in very bad shape—but a man like Plume couldn't be counted out until he lay dead in his grave.

Phin drove himself uphill toward the setting sun. Walking eased the ache in his bones. The fresh breeze carried away the leftover heat of the boxcar and brought a promise of chill. He was thirsty, hungry, and he needed shelter before nightfall. Still, a weight seemed lifted from him. He was out of the boxcar, alone and free.

The trees thinned to open meadow, brown with dry goldenrod. An abandoned farmhouse overlooked it, sway-backed, with glass-less windows. Its dark weathered siding blended with the woods above. Toiling up the slope, Phin found the remnants of a fallen barn, some rotted fence rails, a stone pen—

And at last, what he was looking for. Behind the barn, a tiny stream trickled from a stone pipe in the hillside, dropping musically into a mossy wooden trough. Small, nearly invisible stick things bent and straightened, bent and straightened, in the depths. Phin cupped his hand under the pipe and collected a palmful. No swimmers. It looked clean and clear and it tasted like—

It tasted like water.

When he'd finally had enough, Phin looked around. Could he stay here? It answered two of his needs, water and shelter.

The door stuck, but a gentle shove with his shoulder pushed it open. Dead leaves were deep in the corners of the first room. Rodents rustled. In the next room a table stood near the leaf-filled fireplace, bare except for mouse droppings. The stairs were broken. There seemed no reason to go up.

He stepped outside, away from the mousy smell. The sun had set. No time to look for food, but he could gather some firewood—

Down in the trees a horse snorted.

Phin was behind the house before he knew he'd started running. Past the barn, past the spring; he plunged into the sheltering woods and looked back.

A horse and rider came out into the open. Phin didn't need to see a face. It was Fraser, his hat, his long dark coat, his stallion, coming at a swift walk, head low, snatching bites of grass while Phin stood paralyzed with shock, unable to think, barely able to breathe.

Fraser let the horse eat a moment while he scanned the field, the old house, the fallen barn.

Then he did an odd thing. Drawing the horse's head up, he reached forward and took hold of the bridle by the cheek strap. A moment later the bit dropped out, and swung like a cowbell at the stallion's throat.

Fraser reached back into his saddlebags and took something out. Phin caught a glimpse of gray cloth. Man and horse considered it. Then Fraser put it back in the saddlebag and let the reins go slack.

The stallion gazed uphill, wild head turning as he seemed to search the edge of the woods. When he stopped moving, he was pointing directly at Phin.

Fraser nodded. He picked up the reins and lifted the stallion into a canter, straight up the meadow.

Released from his trance, Phin fled, twisting between trees, ripping through brambles.

An immense crack and rustle behind; the horse had entered the wood. Phin heard a loud snap, a curse from Fraser, and looked wildly over his shoulder. Fraser was drawing rein, coming on at a trot with one arm flung up to protect his face.

"Wait!" he called.

Phin ducked behind a big tree. The stallion charged past, overshooting. Fraser wrenched him around, making up ground with terrifying speed. Phin could see the sweat on Fraser's face. A gloved hand reached. Phin swerved like a weasel. Fraser missed and was carried far past, swearing.

The saplings ahead grew close as the teeth of a comb. Phin shoved through them, and the ground dropped out from under him. He plunged down a slope thick with brown pine needles—somersaulting, hitting rocks and tree trunks so fast, so nearly airborne, that nothing really hurt. Faster and faster, till the ground flattened out and he rolled to a stop.

He lifted his head. Everything spun, and slowly settled. He lay beside a small stream. Pines soared above him. It was almost dark under their green-black roof, as if he'd fallen into another world.

The real world was close, though. Above him he heard hoofbeats. He dragged himself to his feet and ran downstream.

Scrambling sounds came from behind; the stallion must be sliding down the pine slope. Phin tried to look over his shoulder and something hard caught him on the shins. He fell sprawling on an immense rock that lay across the stream. Pushing himself up, he saw wheel ruts on either side. A bridge, low and crude.

Hooves drummed. Phin scrambled off the rock and threw himself full length into the stream.

The water came halfway up his ribs, shockingly cold, but yes, there was space under the great stone. He squirmed in, icy water pooling in the small of his back. There was an old cold smell of dirt and worms.

Was he all the way in? He tried to look back, but couldn't raise or turn his head. He wiggled deeper, till his head was near the other side, clenching his teeth to stop their chattering.

A stone in the streambed dug painfully into his hip. He tried to reach down and move it, and as his elbow struck the rock above, he realized that it wasn't a stone at all. It was his wooden matchbox, soaking in cold water.

He forced his arm back, scraping a channel in the mud; fought his fingers into the pocket; wormed out the matchbox and wad of money; held them, dripping, above the water.

Which was deeper than before, wasn't it? He was ponding the stream behind him—

He felt it then, the little scrape of panic that could so easily grow. The rock seemed to press on him. The water could rise swiftly, he could drown—

He raised himself on elbows and knees. There was barely room, but the water rushed under his chin with a grateful little gurgle and ran free again. Phin breathed deep, felt the rock press his back—

Don't notice that. Wonder instead; was the water flowing out muddy? Would Fraser see?

And where was he? Was he coming? Phin was deaf down here as well as blind—

A thud reverberated through the rock above. The horse. He heard a faint boom that might be a voice. More thudding, then quiet for a long time, so long Phin thought horse and rider were gone for good, so long his teeth started rattling in his head—

Another thump.

Hooves crunched in the streambed, uphill. A smell of mud came on the water.

Sound and smell faded.

Phin waited, until he was shuddering so hard it actually hurt and he knew he had to get out, no matter what.

Still holding his matches and money above water, he squirmed on elbows and knees and stomach, out into the icy air.

The woods were dusky and quiet, empty feeling. Phin could hardly stand for shivering. He clambered out of the streambed and began gathering dry sticks.

Below the bridge a dead pine had fallen across the brook. Its limbs popped like pistol shots when he broke them. If Fraser was near, he'd hear. No choice, though.

There was more than one way to die. He laid his fire with fingers that shook so hard he kept knocking the delicate pile of tinder apart; and at last, with a big knot of fear in him, opened the damp matchbox.

His fingers were almost too numb to count them—four, five, six matches. He pressed one match head to his cheek.

Dry.

He struck it against one of the stones. A small flame leaped in the darkness, pure and golden. Phin touched it to his tinder in a few places, puffed gently with his breath. Suddenly the whole pile took with licking fire. He'd never seen anything more beautiful.

14
ALONE

Phin's eyes snapped open in gray dawn light. He lay
curled under the thin cover of the flour sack, listening. But
if a sound had awakened him, it didn't repeat. The pine
slope was brown and bare. He was alone.

He sat up and stretched, feeling scraped, bruised, hungry, and chilled. His shirt was dryish, his pants not quite so
dry. He'd crouched naked by the fire a long time last night,
feeding it branches, and toasting his belongings on sticks.
Finally he woke to the smell of his pants smoldering,
dressed and curled up for the night.

Another fire would feel good now, but there was nothing to cook. Last night he'd skewered his bacon and sizzled

it up, and it was gone. He had five matches left. He'd need every one of them to get him through—

Through to where? He didn't know where he was, much less what to do next.

Get up. Have a drink. A drink would fill his belly.

He limped to the brook, but water didn't chase away hunger, only made it cold hunger, sloshing hunger.

He brushed dry mud off his clothes, then checked his pockets. Knife, tobacco, matches, money—his hand hesitated over the roll of bills. He was tempted, again, to read the paper. What harm could it do now?

Again something stopped him, almost as physical as a hand on his shoulder. It didn't say why. It just—he just—didn't want that paper read.

Fine. Time to get moving, anyway.

Downhill was the train, was Plume, maybe. Fraser had ridden off upstream. Phin had meant to go uphill himself, but his feet refused to turn that way, and through all this, his body had given him good advice.

So he'd go along the hillside a ways and then head—north, he decided. Farther from coal country.

He climbed up out of the pines. The sun had risen. The leaves glowed and shifted, and a brilliant blue sky showed between them. It was beautiful and the birds sang, and

Phin got warmer as he walked, and yet his heart swelled and ached. He'd always been surrounded by people— some bad, some unreliable, some, lately, enemies. But they'd been there. They'd spoken and laughed. They'd known him, or at least his face. They were his kind; even the groups he didn't fit into: miners, drinkers, chewers, fighters. Irish. English. Better to have people you didn't fit with than no people at all—

At which point his mother gave him a vigorous nudge.

She knew self-pity, and she'd conquered it. Phin had seen her stop sometimes when things were hard—like now—and close her eyes, take a breath. Her face would smooth and soften, seem younger. When she'd open her eyes, they'd be bright and clear again, and she'd look around.

At Murray's back shed, piles of coal-grimed overalls, steaming wash water. But Phin had golden maples in the sun; the singing woods; cool shadows; a mushroom that looked exactly like a small brown dinner roll sprinkled with salt—

His stomach growled.

All right. He was free. Alone and free, and the world was beautiful. Yes, it could have more food in it, but he'd find something if he stayed alert. Meanwhile he could live on this air, maybe. He breathed deep, and deep again, and his blood began to tingle.

At Murray's they'd talked of marches on short rations. Phin had never believed men could walk all day on two weevily biscuits, but look at him now. His father might have gone through something like this—

—his dead father—

—and so had many others, most of whom survived and even fought battles afterward. A person is capable of other states besides the ordinary, and he was passing into one of these, his body faint and thin as a thread, yet moving steadily, lightly through the woods, his mind crystal clear, lines of poetry coming back effortlessly. He couldn't get them wrong. The poems wouldn't let him.

Phin thanked his mother, who'd told him, "You may not always have books, Phinny, but once you learn a poem, you can take it with you anywhere."

She was with him on this journey, even more than in the weeks after her death when, impossibly, he'd kept expecting to hear from her, when he'd look at her bed or chair and be surprised to find it empty.

She'd love all this. She'd sniff the air, toss the leaves to see them twirl and drift, match his poetry line for line. Water ahead, a gurgling stream. Wordsworth whispered, "I love the Brooks which down their channels fret. . . ." Thrush song rose, and robin song, too, all beautiful, varied and loud, and Wordsworth said, "Then sing ye Birds, sing, sing a joyous song!"

Phin paused to pull his belt tighter. They said that gave you the feeling of having eaten. They were wrong; it reminded Phin that he hadn't. He loosened it again and walked on, telling himself each time he saw a strawberry-colored or egg yolk–colored mushroom that he didn't know mushrooms. Mushrooms could kill you. He marched himself past them and on.

And on.

And on.

His feet ached by the time he came to signs of recent logging. His head ached, too, and the exalted feeling was leaving him.

Not this year's logging; maybe last, by the way the undergrowth had sprung up. Another good hike, maybe a half mile, brought the sight of open land ahead.

His feet picked up a run for a few steps, but he was too tired. He walked more quickly, though, seeing as he neared the edge of the wood that it wasn't open land, but a vast growth of bramble.

Blackberries.

Phin stumbled out into the sunshine, already searching. He could tell that there had been berries, many berries.

Only the bare stems were left, and the little dry leaves that crown a berry and sometimes the center cone.

He searched on, because the brambles were still green, they hadn't turned color or started to drop, and a few yards farther—there!

He fell on his knees and grabbed for a glistening fruit, popped it in his mouth. It was perfectly ripe and burst against his tongue, tart and sweet and seedy.

And there were more. They were the last of the crop, hanging high on the drying stems. Birds must have gotten the rest.

He ate, and pushed his way through brambles, and ate more. A berry, even a handful of berries, was nothing. He could never get enough of them.

In one place a great pathway had been trampled. Many berries were crushed and wasted. What could have made it, Phin wondered, grazing along the edge.

Bear. Of course. Bear.

The breakage was at least a week old, by the way the leaves and fruit had dried. The bear must have moved on—

No, *might* have moved on. That was an important distinction, and Phin had finally crammed enough berries into his mouth to make it. He paused to look around and listen.

It was warm in the sunshine. The sky had softened to a

paler, midday blue, and a gentle breeze stirred. The whole place felt lively and friendly and pleasant, and without the least hint of bear; not even—he breathed deep—a scent. Bears stank, didn't they? He didn't know anything about them by actual experience, but they'd figured among tales of daring at Murray's.

He went on picking. Now he was able to leave unripe or overripe fruit hanging, take the largest, most thimble-shaped berries and enjoy each one separately. The spicy juice was better than Murray's wine, better than almost anything Phin had ever eaten—

A sharp sound downhill, like a voice. Phin looked that way, but bushes blocked his view. A crow flew overhead; it must have been the crow he'd heard.

It came again, like a word. "—right," he thought he heard, in a high, clear voice. He looked up at the sky, wait-ing for another crow to cross it.

"—think so?"

A woman's voice. Phin froze behind the bush.

"—minute ago I was slower than God's off ox, and now I'm slower than molasses in January. Which is it?"

" 'A foolish consistency is the hobgoblin of little minds,' " said a girl's clear voice. "And you can't argue with that, because Emerson is always right!"

15
FOLLOWER

Phin peered through the lace of briars.

They weren't as close as they sounded; three women with a spade, pails, and sacks. Each wore a broad-brimmed straw hat. The first two were small and light. The third was broader and walked more slowly, as if her feet hurt.

"Now Mummy, sit!" one of the small ones said—the girl who'd quoted Emerson. "We'll pick, and then you can do the digging. Did you bring your book?"

The larger woman's voice didn't carry, but Phin saw her shake her head as she settled herself on a rock.

"Oh, Mummy! We wanted you to rest!"

"If that was the point, Abby, we've fetched her an awful

long way!" The third voice was an old woman's. The mother reached into her bag and took out some knitting. Abby shook her head and turned away.

"All right, Gran, split up or both together?"

"Together. If we run into that bear—"

"He'll have a choice!" Abby laughed, a bubbling sound like the brooks made. "Which of us do you think makes better eating?"

"You'll be tenderer, but I'll have more flavor, like an old hen. These berries are about played out—I thought there'd be more left." Complaining and searching for the berries Phin had just eaten, they moved rapidly out of earshot.

The mother knitted industriously for a few minutes, then paused to reach into a bag and take out a crockery jug. She drank and sat looking around, hands and knitting at rest in her lap.

Phin saw her shoulders move in a large sigh as she took up her work again. It was pleasant to watch her. She seemed at peace, and Phin had a sudden, uncomfortable awareness of himself, dirty and ragged, spying on her. He should come out and speak—

Something crashed in the bushes off to his left; not close, but moving rapidly. Phin straightened. He was a little behind the woman, out of her line of sight, but he kept his head down, listening. The sound went away.

He crouched again. It felt stupid. He was a respectable person, even if he didn't look that way. Shouldn't he just introduce himself, and ask for help?

It seemed a reasonable question, but he couldn't do it. There was some barrier inside him, as there'd been about reading Plume's paper. These women came from somewhere, possibly the town. Phin had no idea how far he'd traveled from it, if Plume was there, if Fraser was there. He couldn't risk it. Maybe if he listened he could pick up some clue as to where—

The crashing came his way again. Phin stood and turned to face it. Bears—what were you supposed to do? So much tavern talk, all his life; you'd think it would have taught him something useful.

The tops of the brambles waved. Something beneath them snuffled and panted. Then through the tangle burst a medium-sized brown dog.

At the sight of Phin, its eyes bulged. The hair ridged on its back and it barked.

"Shh!" Phin waved his hands frantically. The dog barked harder.

"Mum?" Abby called from a long way off.

"It's all right," her mother answered calmly. "Lucky has something cornered, I guess."

"A bear?"

"I doubt it."

"Lucky, come here! *Lucky!* Stupid dog—"

Phin picked up a clod of dirt and threw. It connected; Lucky yipped and drew another call from Abby.

Her voice emboldened the dog. He dashed at Phin, nipping at his pants, bounced back and lunged again. Retreating, Phin tripped and sprawled on his back.

He sprang up, snatching the stout branch he'd fallen over. Lucky gave it a comprehending look and circled, growling, then barked again when Phin sidled toward the woods.

"*Lucky!* LUCKY!"

After four or five more barks, Lucky abruptly turned, as if satisfied he'd gotten the last word, and trotted off.

Phin was left a short distance from the trees, surrounded on all sides by the eye-level tangle of brambles. The quiet felt like food after hunger, water after thirst; like the woods after the train. He could hear the crows again, real crows this time, and the women greeting Lucky. They must be all together again, talking, voices fading—

With a jolt he realized they were leaving.

He mustn't lose them. Gripping his stick, he slipped

through the brambles and along the bear trail, picking up the voices again. He expected to come to a waiting horse and buggy, but when he got to where he could see them, there was no vehicle in sight.

They were at the edge of the briar patch now. Poplar saplings rimmed the sky, leaves shivering. The mother was digging at the base of a bramble while Abby tugged with gloved hands. The grandmother, also gloved, was putting a just-pulled bramble into a sack. Lucky sat watching.

After a moment his nose lifted. Phin saw the tiny motions of his head as he tested the breeze. Bristling, he turned toward Phin and barked.

"Lucky, enough!" The old woman grabbed for him; he eluded her, but Abby dived on him, startling out a yip. She held him with one arm while she unfastened her apron and tied the strings around his neck. Then she led him to the grandmother, who stood firmly on the dragging fabric. All the while Lucky barked.

The mother wiped her forehead with the back of her wrist and said something to the grandmother, who cupped an ear at her.

"I said—we won't get up here again soon! I want to get enough." She turned toward Phin, brandishing her shovel. "Get out of here! Scoot!"

Did she see him? Phin froze, realizing too late that it would have been smart to crash away, as an animal would.

The three worked quickly, glancing over their shoulders. The mother pried at the blackberry roots, Abby hauled them out, the grandmother shoved them into bags. All the while she stared in Phin's direction. Phin was too far away to see her features, but that face turned his way was a threat, a warning.

At last they were done. They gathered up buckets and sacks and hurried downhill. Lucky, hauled along by Abby, twisted his head around and raved over his shoulder.

They must live nearby, then. Phin hadn't dared hope for that; a house, farm animals, a garden. He stood up to follow, letting Lucky's noise guide him. He could pick up what he needed; food, a water bottle—

Pick up? the inconvenient voice within asked.

Phin touched the roll of cash in his pocket. Okay, buy— though these were large bills. It would be a lot to pay for the few things he hoped to take. He could hardly ask for change, though.

Wrestling with conscience, he followed them down an old wagon road; shallow wheel ruts grown over with thin, silky grass. The road began to look more used as it passed under large maples. A stone wall ran along one side, a brook on the other. Below him now Phin saw a roof, then the gray walls of barn and house, a cow at pasture and—his heart thumped—a dark horse.

It wore no saddle or bridle, was grazing peacefully, and was, as he got close enough to see, a mare; not a bad one, though not of the quality of Fraser's stallion. She raised her head, chewing, to watch the berrying party, then pricked her ears uphill as if sensing the follower.

The warning went unheeded. Mother, grandmother, and dog disappeared inside. The girl spread the blackberry plants on a rock in the sun. Then she, too, vanished into the house. Phin crept closer, to the corner of the stone wall that divided the uphill pasture from the farmyard, and looked the place over.

It was a large house, and the barn seemed large, too, but both were shabby. Phin could tell no man lived here. Oh, there might be a male invalid inside, or an ancient grandfather. But so many jobs had been left unfinished, unbegun, or improvised. The front door sagged. The garden fence was mended with a section of iron bedstead. The cow was staked, not pastured. The mare was lame; no need to pasture her, and a good thing because there was no pasture fence, just a few weathered rails atop the stone wall to show there'd been one once. The hens weren't penned either, but scratched in the yard.

Hens. Eggs.

And chicken—roast chicken, fried chicken, chicken pie . . . the plump hens, live and crooning as they were, made Phin's stomach growl. As if in response came a suspicious bark from inside the house.

Phin slunk back to higher ground. He found a maple with a low branch and settled there to watch, like a fox watching a henhouse. He didn't relish the feeling. He'd been brought up to help and respect women. But food. He had to have food.

He was jerked from a reverie—chicken and biscuit, chicken fricassee—by the sound of a train whistle.

It could be any train. It could even be doing him good, carrying Plume back to Bittsville or Fraser to wherever he might be going—if he'd given up the hunt; if either of them had given up. But this little farm road connected to some other road downhill and another after that, to the valley and the railroad and coal country. He must feed himself and move on, quickly.

The sun edged closer to the hill. A breeze came up. The old lady appeared, visited the outhouse, split a little kindling rather handily with a hatchet, and went back inside.

A few minutes later smoke puffed from the chimney.

Lucky was put out; probably interfering with supper preparations. He sniffed around the yard and backtracked uphill the way they'd all come, bristling when he came to where Phin had turned around. He raised his head and woofed several times, staring hard in the wrong direction. The breeze was coming uphill from the yard, not downhill toward the dog. After a while, with a sort of huff, Lucky turned to other business.

Now Abby came out with a pail. She reached through the barn door and took down a faded blue army coat, buttoned it over her clothes, and walked out to the cow. By clenching his fist and looking at her through the smallest opening he could make, Phin brought her into focus; a small person with regular, determined features, pretty in an unextravagant way. He couldn't tell if she was his age or a little older. She seemed like someone who had come into her looks and wouldn't change much from now on.

Down on one knee in the grass, she pressed her forehead against the cow's flank. Phin imagined the milk filling the pail—white, sweet smelling, warm, and frothy. He could take it, drink it all down. How could she stop him?

Lucky could probably stop him.

After milking, she set the pail aside, pulled up the stake,

and moved the cow to fresh grass, tempting her along with a treat—something white, a piece of bread maybe, or a slice of turnip. Phin wanted it, whatever it was. He wanted the cow, too. His thoughts ran on pickled beef and beef tea and steak and stew. . . .

Abby carried the pail back, pausing to hang the coat up. She hugged herself briefly as the cool air struck her. Phin wished she hadn't. He'd managed to ignore the growing cold. The sun had set, taking the warmth with it.

Abby went into the house and came out wrapped in a shawl. She sat on the bench by the door and took a sock on four needles out of her apron pocket, spread a book open beside her, and bent, reading fiercely, as if this was the moment she'd waited for all day. She knitted, too. Phin saw the moment when it was shawl fringe instead of sock yarn that her busy fingers worked. She only noticed when the shawl began to pull at her neck. Then she tugged the fringe loose impatiently and crushed the sock in her lap, reading on.

Phin wanted the shawl and what was cooking in the kitchen. He wanted the book, too. What was it? Had he read it? He wanted to look over her shoulder. He wanted her to go inside and leave it on the bench.

Lucky scrounged around the foundations, sniffing for mice.

Tender little morsels, mice—

Finally the mother came out to the front step. A brief exchange; Phin couldn't hear it, but it was perfectly clear. Abby wanted to read more. Her mother thought it was too dark. Besides, supper was ready.

They put on gloves and carried the wilting blackberry canes into the barn. What were they doing? Phin wondered. Those plants wouldn't live now with the roots dried out—

But blackberry root bark was an infallible cure for diarrhea. They'd been harvesting medicine on the hill, he realized, the way people did at home.

The house door shut behind them. Phin slid out of the tree. Time to make his move.

16
PHIN AGAIN

First he drank from the brook. Then Phin walked down the farm road through the deepening shadows. The horse lifted her head as he passed.

He climbed the wall that divided yard from field, and crossed silently to the garden. It was near the end of the house, overlooked by two dark windows. The house seemed cold and lonely at this end.

But at the corner where house and barn connected, yellow lamplight glowed. A river of scent drifted Phin's way; fried apples and onions; salt pork. His mouth flowed with saliva. He pushed open the garden gate.

It was nearly dark, the world all sepia colored like a

brown old photograph. Phin made out a stand of currant bushes, and rows of plants he didn't recognize. Brushed with his hands they gave off medicinal aromas; some sharp and fresh, like mint and lavender, others dark and musky and powerful.

There was a row of turnips, half a row of greens. He broke off a leaf and crunched it—kale, maybe? A long patch of dug-up ground must have held potatoes. He groped in the dirt for a few minutes, but found only stones.

He inventoried the rest: a tall plant with spines; several patches that looked bare, but released an herbal smell when stepped on; a squadron of dry cornstalks shivering in the breeze. Frost had hit this garden already. Back home they were talking about when it might come.

Phin unwrapped his flour sack from around his neck, stepped in among the corn, and took hold of a long ear. It cracked loudly when he tried to break it loose. The house didn't seem to notice, but Phin felt uneasy. He got out Dennis's knife and cut it off, dropped it in his sack.

He took only two more, because he didn't know how he'd eat them. The kernels were hard as pebbles. Maybe he could crush them between two stones, but he'd still have to cook them somehow. Vivid in his mind were tales from Murray's of things soldiers had been driven to eat, and the consequences. He couldn't afford to cripple himself with dysentery.

But turnip was good raw. Murray used to snack on it, rather than the salty, thirst-making free lunch he provided for his customers. With a pang of homesickness almost as sharp as his hunger, Phin remembered the calm bulk behind the bar, the steady, disillusioned eyes, the crunch of crisp raw turnip and the big paw holding out a slice to him, just a little boy then. . . .

He wrenched a large turnip out of the ground. The crushed greens gave off a spicy scent, and he gobbled one with its seasoning of grit.

Two, three, four turnips; into the bag.

His hands tingled with cold by now, and he was shivering. He let himself out of the garden, closing the gate, and moved toward the buildings.

"—good thing the mare's lame," said the grandmother as he passed the kitchen window. Her voice was small through the glass. "If we'd taken her up there today, she'd have likely run off—"

"And lamed herself!" Abby said. "Yes, Mr. Emerson!"

Phin paused, arrested. This was how he and his mother had talked, Emerson and Wordsworth joining them over the washtubs like uncles.

"It's not Emerson's best essay," the old woman said, a little stiffly, "but I've found it useful to walk around a thing and see it from the other side. Just now I'm trying to see the other side of your sass!"

"Sass, Gran? That's just my erect soul, inspiring all beholders with some of my own nobility."

"The devil can quote scripture to his own purposes," the old woman said, while Phin struggled to place Abby's quotation. The essay was "Heroism," and the line Phin remembered from it ran something like this: "The hero doesn't ask to dine nicely and sleep warm." Outside the window, cold to the marrow and bathed in the smell of fried onion, he had to smile.

Ask them for help. Why not? Just knock on the door and explain. Yes, his sack was heavy with their turnips and corn, but he meant to pay. If he came to the door, if he confessed freely, might he be forgiven?

He could imagine the scene, but couldn't make himself knock, not until he knew how close the town was and if it harbored recently arrived strangers. Shivering, he skirted the pale rectangle of lamplight on the ground and made for the black opening of the barn door.

He reached in as the girl had, and his fingers brushed good army wool. Many a coat like this had come home from the war. They were hard for his mother to see and launder, but when Phin put the coat on, he felt at home.

He was warm almost at once, but it was more than that. While he stood waiting for his eyes to adjust, something else adjusted. He felt like Phin again, not a wolfish skulker. A small change; he was still hungry and desperate, with a sack full of food he hadn't paid for yet and no idea what to do next. But the coat put him together, made him whole.

His eyes adjusted to the deeper dark. He could see the things on the wall. A bottle; one sniff told him, horse linament. A can of pine tar, not, so far as he knew, edible. Harness. Ropes, skillfully coiled and hung. Dennis had taught him that, to loop the last bit around the coil and make a slipknot, and another knot in the very end to hang it by. "Don't just ball it up and throw it at the wall!" he could hear the old man say.

Rope might be useful. He chose a piece small enough to fit in the pocket of the coat.

There was a grain bin. Phin opened it, ready for mice, but the bin had a clean smell. It must be tight and well sealed. Way down in the bottom he found oats, not a large supply. He put a handful in his mouth and a couple more in the flour sack.

That was all for this wall. On the other side were three

stalls with hay stored above them, piled high like an extravagant thatch. He saw several hens up there, dark plump shapes. He reached, but the hay was well above his head.

He felt his way along the wall and found a ladder, securely nailed straight up and down. Sack in his teeth, he swarmed up and dived one hand under a hen, seizing her warm legs. She flapped her wings and squawked bloody murder. Phin lunged, pinning her under his elbow, muffling her in the coat, and with his fingers on her silken-feathered throat, hesitated.

He could kill her, but then he couldn't stay. He'd need to quickly find a place where he could pluck and gut her before the meat spoiled.

He relaxed his grip. The hen fluttered a few feet away, setting up a murmur and crooning among the others.

In the morning, Phin thought.

He turned away, crawling across the hay toward the back of the mow. Trapping himself again, but this time no Fraser lurked below, no Plume. The women weren't a threat. If he was discovered, he could walk right past them.

Or he could ask—

His hand came down on something small and smooth. He knew what it was, but couldn't stop in time. Eggshell crunched. He recoiled, expecting a cloud of stench.

But this egg was fresh, not rotten. Only a smell of wetness came, and before Phin knew what he was doing he'd put his head down, slurping thick mellow yolk and slippery white. Eggshell gritted in his teeth. Wetness and chaff stuck to his chin. Part of him was shocked; but haste was needed, or the hay would soak up the egg, and haste kept him from gagging.

As he finished, the house door opened. A moment later Lucky gave a suspicious woof. He roamed the yard, making comments, and finally began barking in the barn doorway. Phin crouched with his back to the wall and waited.

"Lucky?" Abby called. Lucky barked in answer; an officious dog, Phin felt, a busybody.

"Remember the boy who cried wolf, Lucky!"

"Remember the skunk!" her grandmother said, and Phin heard the little yelp he'd come to know, a scrabble of paws as Lucky was towed toward the house.

"Do you suppose something followed us off the hill?" the mother asked. "A bobcat'll do that, I've heard."

"He was quiet all afternoon," Abby said. "He's not the most reliable dog, Mummy, you know that."

"All the same, shall we go out together?"

Out? Oh. Outhouse.

Lantern light wandered out into the darkness. Dry

leaves swooshed. Lucky barked inside the house. After several minutes the three came back, chatting quietly. "I declare," the mother said, "that moon's almost bright enough to read by, Abby." Abby said something through a yawn, and the door closed behind them. Soon the rectangle of lamplight on ground puffed out.

Early to bed; though if Phin knew that girl, and he was beginning to feel he did, she was lighting another lamp somewhere and opening her book.

Phin wouldn't have minded a book himself. He'd plumbed the depths of solitude and his own company. But he had his turnips. He crunched more greens, making as much noise in the quiet barn as a stabled horse eating hay; rubbed dirt off one turnip with a handful of hay, and carved slices with his knife. Fresh, spicy, the turnips were a feast. After a while he even felt full.

And comfortable, in the warm coat and soft hay. He pulled more hay over him, making a deep bed, and took a handful of oats from the sack. Dessert.

He should make a plan now. At least start thinking what to do, where to go. How to pay. Tuck a bill under that bottle.

Outside an owl hooted. Another answered, a long way off, and in the barn a mouse squeaked, and . . .

❖ ❖ ❖ ❖ ❖

ERRRRRR!

Phin leaped up. Pale light, gray-gold mounds of hay. On the beam in front of him a rooster swelled its chest, threw its head back, and bellowed a challenge to the dawn.

Phin sank down, nerves twanging. Hens dropped off the beams around him. Some flapped to the floor below. Others strolled across the hay, clucking and pecking and seeking secluded corners.

No sound from the house yet. Phin put his eye to a crack between the barn boards. All he could see was tree-tops, gold and green and scarlet, sloping downhill under a pearly sky.

Apparently he hadn't made a plan last night. Apparently he'd fallen asleep instead.

Now what? He rubbed his face hard with both hands, trying to wake up all the way.

Off in a corner, one hen began a raucous squawking. A few minutes later another joined in. With a last yawn and vigorous headshake, Phin got his mind to work.

Eggs. They were laying eggs.

He went to where the first hen was singing her own praises, boosted her gently out of the way, and palmed the warm egg into his pocket. He waited for the next announcement, and the next, and nestled the eggs in the coils of rope—four in all.

Now grab a bird and go, while the house was quiet. One hen still sat on her nest near the front of the mow. He started toward her, steeling himself and trying to quiet his conscience, troubled by the idea of interrupting the poor creature. He could wait, but he might wait too long, and it was a strange quibble. After all, he did plan to murder her.

The house door opened.

No time to get out of sight. Quick footsteps approached the barn doorway, and Abby came in.

Her hair was rough and uncombed, her eyes puffy with sleep. She reached for the coat without looking. For a long moment her hand stretched and felt for what it knew was there.

Her head turned. She stared at the empty peg and the floor below it. Then she looked up, and met Phin's eyes.

His heart didn't stop; he could hear his own pulse thunder in his ears. It was the world that seemed to stop, while the face below him paled, the eyes widened and darkened.

She whirled, with a swish of skirts. "Mum, the gun! There's someone in the barn!"

17
THE LAST EGG

The word *gun* sent Phin running, without thought or hesitation. Down the ladder, sliding, skipping rungs; out the barn door and around the back, in a flurry of impressions—dresses bunched near the house, shouts. "Get in here!" "Lucky, no!" "Grab him!" Barks and thumps.

A grove of sumac trees flashed past. A rock-strewn slope fell away under him. Phin jumped down it, wide reckless leaps, with Lucky shrill at his heels. A tug at his pant leg; Lucky's teeth—

He whirled, and Lucky skidded, eyes bulging, and drew back—a coward as well as a loudmouth. Phin looked for a rock, but they were all too big, grown into the sod. He took an egg from his pocket, threw it at Lucky—

Missed. The egg splatted yellow on the ground.

Lucky's ears went forward. His nose wrinkled, sniffing. He approached the egg warily, but with great interest. Phin looked wildly uphill.

He could see the peak of the barn above the treetops. Everything else was screened off by brush. He was already in another world—an old pasture rimmed with stone walls and growing up to saplings and junipers. Though he could hear Abby's voice clearly—calling Lucky, worried; she liked the dog better she let on—she seemed far off.

Delicately, Lucky began to lap at the egg. "Lucky, come!" Abby cried, and then—"No, Gran! You'll hit him!"

Phin took one long walking step, another, watching Lucky over his shoulder. The dog ignored him, busy with his egg.

Phin took off running, only it felt more like flying, the hill was so steep. It tipped him down faster and faster, till he hit level ground at the bottom with a jolt that almost dropped him.

He paused to look back. Lucky was trotting uphill, licking his chops. He could see a bit of house roof now, a pair of windows like watching eyes—

He ran again, leaping a juniper, dodging a woodchuck hole. Cold air sawed at his throat. Make it to the stone wall at the bottom of the field. He could hide behind that for a moment, catch his breath.

As he got closer he saw, below the wall, a graveyard, dark slate markers in tilting rows. The walls that ran everywhere across these woods and fields came together here to make a small square pen, the land within it sunken. Phin swung himself over the wall, cradling the egg pocket, and dropped down among the graves.

From this side the wall was chest high. He leaned against it, hands on knees, breath coming in sobs. He was hidden here; safe, for a moment.

When he'd gotten enough air, when he was only breathing hard, he turned to look uphill at the empty field, the buildings showing above the treetops trim and sound, like prosperity defined.

Prosperous. The opposite of how Phin felt. He patted the coat, trying to account for an empty-handed feeling. He'd lost something, forgotten something—

Oh.

The flour sack. His turnips, his corn, his handfuls of oats. In the hay, next to where he'd slept.

Well.

Oh well.

Well, he was lucky. He still had the eggs.

Unbelievably lucky.

Better eat them soon, or he'd end up licking them out of the coat pocket.

He turned from the sight of house and barn, from thoughts of hens and turnips, and looked at the gravestones.

He could make out a face atop one, with wings where the ears should be. The shallow, flowing letters were mostly unreadable, though one name recurred everywhere: Collins. This must be a family graveyard. That meant town was faraway. Otherwise wouldn't they bury their people there?

In the center of the plot was a newer stone, not slate, but granite, large, thick, and polished. The words on it were readable even from a distance: "Randal Collins, 1830–1864 Beloved Son, Husband, Father."

There were more words, smaller letters. Phin went closer and the stone stated, "He died to make men free."

That was from "The Battle Hymn of the Republic." *"As He died to make men holy let us die to make men free"*—The back of Phin's neck prickled. Without a doubt, he stood at this grave in the man's own coat.

He almost took it off. Leave it folded on the grave, that was the right thing to do, with the rope and the three eggs on top of it, and move on.

But something steadied him, even as his fingers worked at a button. The stones stood still around him. *Easy, boy,* they seemed to say. No hurry.

He looked around with eyes that felt freshly opened. A little path was worn from the gate to Randal Collins's grave. A dent in the sod, an old dent; grass had grown to cover it and had not been trampled this season.

"*A child said,* What is the grass? *fetching it to me with full hands;—*"

Phin looked up at the pearly sky. He drew a deep breath, full of the spice-scent of the brilliant leaves, and he remembered the sun rising through John Engelbreit's front door as he surfaced from that poem.

He was part of everything, and everything was part of him. That was what he'd felt, reading through that night and in those few moments when the door stood open. The grass was alive with meaning and so was he, and nothing was dead. No one was dead, not these Collinses all in rows, not Engelbreit. Everything was different than what people supposed, Whitman said. It was better—

And he should think. It was time to think.

With utmost control, he dented the end of an egg on the stone, pried shell fragments out of the shallow crater he had made, and through the tiny opening sucked the thick liquid. And considered.

He'd allowed himself to be driven from the beginning, by Plume and Fraser, and now Lucky and that word "gun."

This could go on a long time. The country was broad and wild and men disappeared into it, running from the past.

But if he let himself be driven to the margins of society—another egg—for a crime he hadn't done, Phin knew he would regret it. He'd grown up in a barroom. He knew the margins. He wasn't attracted to them.

So—time to stop running. Time to walk uphill, fold this coat over his arm, and knock on the Collinses' door and apologize, tell his story. He dreaded it, he dreaded the gun and their eyes and the questions, which would be sharp, but in the end he'd get his knees under a table again, he'd get properly fed and properly clean, and respectable people would help him think things through.

He crushed the second eggshell in his hand, dropped it outside the wall, and was reaching for the third—because what if they didn't feed him?—when a sound caught his attention: hoofbeats, crunching on dirt.

The farm road passed just outside the gate. Phin ducked behind Randal Collins's stone as a lank horse came into view, pulling a buggy. He couldn't see the driver, just a pair of hands flicking the reins at the laboring animal.

Behind the buggy, the stallion making the hill seem light work, rode Fraser.

Phin's legs weakened. He dropped to his knees, hot all over, and then cold. How had Fraser found this place? Through the screen of leaves and branches he watched the turning wheels, the stallion's legs, slender and springing, Fraser's boot heels and the tail of his long coat. Up the hill they went, disappearing behind the trees.

The moment they were out of sight, Phin sprinted across the graveyard and vaulted the downhill wall, out into another brushy pasture. Run. Run.

Over his pounding feet he heard Lucky bark far off. Had they reached at the farm already? The women would tell—their alarm was fresh. Abby could describe him—

He was exposed again, out in the open, but at the bottom of the pasture ran another stone wall and beyond it, woods. Phin put on a burst of speed and threw himself over the wall with what felt like the last of his strength. He turned to look back.

The gable end of the house stood high above the

treetops, dominating the hillside like a fort. Lucky was barking, and—

—did he really hear that? He held his breath.

Yes. Something large was crashing downhill. In a moment he made out a dark shape moving beneath the sumacs.

Fraser. The stallion.

The horse's head was low as he picked his way down the rocky slope. Fraser sat easily, leaning back, scanning the pastures.

Phin couldn't look away. The horse's oily, supple motion mesmerized him. He should be running, but he was afraid to make a sound, and anyway he couldn't, not until he got his breath and the weakness went out of his legs.

The stallion kept coming. Phin found himself reaching into his pocket for the last egg. There might be time, just time, to eat it. One way or another it could be a while before he ate again.

Like a soldier watching the start of a distant enemy charge, braced, heart beating light and rapid, he tapped the pointed end of the egg on the wall. He was proud of having the self-control to do this perfectly, not tap too hard, not waste the only food he had. He sucked, and watched.

Horse and rider reached the more level part of the pasture, but the stallion didn't lift his head. He still seemed to seek his way carefully, pausing only at one small juniper and circling it, a bit later zigging around a mound of dirt—

The woodchuck hole. Phin had dodged it. Now the horse dodged it, too, and came straight down the hill to the cemetery wall exactly where Phin had.

He raised his head, sniffing the stones where Phin had swung over. Fraser turned him in a circle and put him at the wall. He jumped it, mane and tail and Fraser's long coat flying, and landed among the graves.

It was the stallion tracking him. He was being followed by his smell.

18
BEAVER DAM

In one of those moments out of time, thoughts outpacing events, Phin sensed the envelope of scent around him; sweat and hay and old wool coat, mud, crushed grass, body heat. Wherever he went he left traces on the air, as continual as candle smoke, as individual as a signature.

The stallion moved among the tombstones. Phin whirled, trying to see and think and run all at the same time. Deeper into the woods—Fraser was a whole field away, so he didn't worry about noise—just space, just go. He wasn't fast enough, didn't have a big enough lead, couldn't keep this up. Tree trunks flashed past. Amazing. No strength, but he was running anyway.

Brush ahead. It might slow the horse, and he zigzagged through it, but how did he muddle a scent trail? He'd read *Uncle Tom*—bloodhounds in that. But a horse wasn't a hound. He hadn't even known they could do this. Could they do this?

The stallion was doing it.

A stone wall. He raced precariously along the top like the fox fleeing dogs, slipped, banged his good shin, paused to listen.

Nothing?

Wind?

Or distant hoofbeats?

Go. Go.

Bitter thoughts ran with him. All the time he'd spent stroking the stallion, the oats he'd given, his hands under the flaring nostrils, as if he'd been trying to imprint his scent in his pursuer's memory.

Had the stallion known he was in the wagon? In the railcar?

Of course, and so had Fraser. Fool! It seemed so clear now. How could he have missed it? When he coughed, and Fraser led the horse in circles, covering the sound; when he said "he's here," mischievously echoing Plume's words. Then why had he done nothing? *Why?*

Phin leaped down a slope. Another little brook; this one trickled out of a deep ravine in the hillside. What else did foxes do? They had tricks for eluding hounds—

Water. Phin ran up the brook into the dark closet of rock.

If Fraser knew he was in the railcar—he'd known!—then why did he keep quiet? Why was he following Phin at all? He didn't believe the tale of Engelbreit's murder—didn't seem to . . .

Up and up the dark slot. It grew deeper, the sides too steep for a horse to climb. Get out here, then, confuse the trail some more. A tree root reached down, as if offering a friendly arm. Phin wrapped his hand around it and hung with all his weight, testing. It held, and he scrambled up.

Higher than he'd thought.

Don't look down.

He elbowed his way onto a bald rock ridge, his whole body scraping earth. That would leave a big scent, but maybe the horse would never get up here to find it. Maybe he'd been clever enough.

He was hot in the coat, reeking with sweat. Wonderful! But if he left the coat, he'd be cold at night, and if he took it off, he'd have to carry it. He unbuttoned it instead, and stood up and flapped the hot air away from his body—

Did Fraser want the paper? Want Phin as a witness? Or did he believe the murder story after all?

Listen.

Something trampling? Or was that his pulse, gushing in his ears?

No. Something out there. Coming.

He turned all the way around once, determined to keep thinking, not run in panic.

There was only one obvious way to go; along the ridge he'd just climbed onto. It ran parallel to the hillside. This seemed to be the low end. Ahead it bulged higher, and Phin was reluctant to go up. He didn't feel strong enough for climbing.

But the rock was almost bare up there. Less vegetation to catch his scent. It was really the only choice, and it turned out he could climb. He always had more strength than he thought. He moved swiftly, stepping over moss patches, trying to walk only on the balls of his feet.

That cloth Fraser held under the stallion's nose—his jacket? Had to be; left in the Sleeper's hands when he fled after Engelbreit's murder.

How did Fraser get it?

How *did* Fraser get it? How did he come into things? Was he a lawman? Coal and Iron Police? Pinkerton detective?

Or a free agent, out for his own advantage? The country was full of men like that, set loose by the war. They'd come back readier to kill, his mother said, and some didn't come back at all, but took to roaming.

What would a man like that want with Phin Chase?

That was easy. Money. A reward—from the Sleepers, maybe, or the owners, or the Pinkertons. That meant he couldn't let Plume in on the capture. He'd needed to get rid of Plume first; then snatch Phin and settle in to bargain. So he'd waited—a man with a dangerous degree of self-control. Phin must have the same. Think.

The horse had scented him in the air. He pictured the stallion gazing uphill at him, nostrils flaring.

So he should think about wind. The wind had hidden him from Lucky; it could hide him now.

He licked a finger and held it up. It got cold on the right, the uphill side. The wind was blowing across his line of flight, and that was good, maybe.

He continued in the same direction, testing the wind whenever he stopped to catch his breath. The overcast was burning off. Misty-blue patches of sky showed between the leaves. All seemed quiet behind, but he didn't believe in quiet anymore, didn't believe he'd shaken off pursuit.

The trees thinned. There was more light, brilliant,

mirrored light. Phin went toward it, noticing dead trees now, and pointed tree stumps, a broad pond, logs on the ground, their tops drowned in the water. Other dead trees rose out of the pond, black and truncated. It was a scene of desolation, but around the shore the living trees flared vivid red and orange.

This must be a beaver pond. Phin had never seen one. As with so much else, he knew them from talk at Murray's. Upstream, brush closed thick around a slow brook. Downstream he glimpsed another dam, maybe two, gently descending like terraces.

Had the beavers abandoned this pond? How would you tell? He listened. Hardly any birds, even; just rustling cattails and the lap of tiny waves at the shore.

A heap of sticks in the middle of the pond drew his eye. That must be the lodge. The beavers had built it and lived inside, getting in through underwater entrances. It looked like a fort out there, surrounded by green glittering water—

Phin shivered in his sweat inside the heavy coat. His body knew what he was going to do. His mind took its time coming to conclusions.

A horse couldn't cross a beaver dam, right? Too heavy. Whereas a man on foot could.

And water deadened scent, right?

And out there in the water was a fort, ready made.

Right?

He shuddered. Was this neccessary? There was no sound behind him, no sound at all—

But there was something below the level of sound, like a pulse on the air—and if he was going to do this, it would take time. He couldn't wait until he was sure. That would be too late.

He made his way toward the dam. Muck and bog guarded the approach. Reluctantly Phin took off his boots.

He hadn't wanted to know how bad his socks were. He hadn't wanted to disturb things or even think about his good luck. No blisters. His barefoot years had stood him in good stead. Until he worked for Dennis, he'd rarely worn shoes in warm weather, and the soles of his feet were tough as a blacksmith's leather apron. But "Bare feet and horses don't mix," Dennis had said, and his mother had gotten him good work boots, knitted him good socks—

Which reeked. He imagined the smell like a firebell clanging through the woods. Quickly he stuffed socks in boots, tied his laces together, and hung his boots around his neck.

Trying to step only on sticks, to leave no track, he

approached the dam. His feet were hot and red. They liked the first feel of sun-warm, shallow water.

But as it got deeper—he rolled up his pant legs—it got colder. His ankles ached. He wanted to hurry, but bare gnawed sticks poked up everywhere. He had to be careful, go slow.

Out along the dam now. Abandoned or not, it was still solid. Sticks and packed mud created a firm surface that hardly gave under his weight. Pointy and scratchy, though. He took a moment to slip his boots back on, and listen.

Yes, there was something.

He made his way as quickly as possible to the middle of the dam, took off coat, shirt, boots, pants, and rolled the coat around everything to make a bundle, tied it tight with the Collinses' rope.

Naked in the sun, he squatted and dug into the dam. The sticks were wedged tight, but he made an opening and stuffed the bundle in, pulling sticks back over it as best he could.

And now.

Phin stared at the chill green water. Solid as a moated castle, the lodge gleamed in the sun. His skin crawled. But something was coming closer, crashing in the distant trees.

He crouched, slipping and wincing on the sticks, and

pushed himself off gently, trying to make barely a ripple.

It was as cold as it looked. Phin's skin sizzled. His wrists ached. His breath came in sobs. But he swam without a sound, hands and feet never breaking the surface. The lodge seemed no nearer, but when he looked back he was twenty feet from the dam, and when he looked at the lodge again, he could see a grass stem growing on it. He kept going, finally gliding onto the back side of the mound.

He was crying by then. Just plain crying, no other word for it. He crawled out of the water and collapsed on the sun-warmed sticks. They scratched and poked the soft parts of his body, but the blessing was that he couldn't feel it much. His skin seemed far away from him, thickened and pimpled like cured pigskin. His hands were blue, his fingers barely flexed, his teeth rattled. Only his tears were warm, trickling down his face and onto his arm.

Soon, though, the approaching sounds grew loud enough to draw his attention.

He didn't take the risk of looking, just listened to the trample as the horse neared the shoreline. There was a pause, and then the crack and snap of breaking sticks coming through the muck toward the dam.

Suddenly he could see the stallion's head. Phin shifted, putting more lodge between himself and his pursuers.

They were at the beginning of the dam. Fraser would have to tie the horse and walk out if he thought Phin had gone that way.

For a long time there was quiet. The sun heated Phin's back. His goose bumps subsided, and the breeze raised more. Wave reflections shimmered on the sticks in front of him.

What was Fraser doing? Moving? Not soundlessly. He'd have to take the stallion back and tie him—

Maybe not.

Phin had to know. He eased himself toward the top of the lodge to risk a quick look. But just below the crown he saw a peephole, a looser place in the interlaced branches. Peering through it, he saw Fraser on the stallion, reins slack. His hat brim slowly turned as he looked up the pond, down the pond.

The stallion's head turned, too. Phin saw the bit sway below the curved black throat. He remembered that from the chase in the woods. Why? Did a bit somehow spoil the sense of smell?

Time passed. Fraser's patience was chilling. Had Phin not found this eyehole, he would have peeked over the lodge by now. Fraser would have seen him. The skill, the unrelenting persistance, seemed professional. Pinkerton.

Had to be. The detective agency's emblem flashed in Phin's mind—a single wide eye and the motto "We Never Sleep. . . ."

Fraser dismounted. He did something to the noseband and the stallion drank, ripples spreading out from his muzzle to lap eventually against the beaver lodge. The horse lifted his head and drops fell back into the shimmering water.

Fraser took a canteen off the saddle. He drank long, then squatted and filled it again. He refastened the canteen to the saddle, put the bit in the stallion's mouth, then mounted and sat another while, still looking. The stallion laid his ears back, and lashed his tail. Phin heard the hiss of it all the way out at the lodge. The animal was impatient; not Fraser.

At last he stood in the stirrups. He cupped both gloved hands around his mouth, wide like the bell of a horn.

"Boy!" His voice rang across the water. "Quit running! I can help you."

19

THIN DARK LINE

Phin's heart rolled over in his chest.

He came so close to standing up that he saw himself doing it, naked, mouth open in astonishment atop the beaver lodge. Sticks dug into his knees and palms as he began to push up.

The words echoed in his mind: *I can help you.*

Can. Not will.

He sank back, pulse beating rapidly in his throat. He felt his own bareness. All his possessions were on the dam, across a stretch of cold water. The only thing he had was his wits.

Had he just taken leave of them? The man said he'd help—

Said he *could* help.

He took a breath, and counted his advantages. The solid mass of beaver lodge was between him and Fraser. So was the wide green water. Even though Fraser knew he was here—

But maybe he didn't. Phin had felt seen, but he was probably meant to feel that way, relax his guard and show himself.

Anyway, how could Fraser know? The breeze was carrying his scent away. Even his clothes, reeking of Phin Chase, were downwind. He was well-washed and well-concealed. Fraser didn't look committed to staying. He was ready to go, rolling the dice one last time to see what happened.

Nothing happened. Phin's not-answering seemed to vibrate the air. A person who really wanted to help would say more, try harder. A person who wanted to *really* help wouldn't have pursued him so relentlessly. He'd have said something earlier. He'd have made himself a lot less frightening. The best Phin could imagine was that Fraser wanted to help him into the witness chair. It might as well be the gallows.

Fraser touched the reins to the stallion's neck. The horse whirled with a snort and surged toward the woods;

jouncing Fraser on purpose, Phin thought, expressing his annoyance—

Fraser wheeled the horse abruptly, staring straight at the lodge. Phin ducked, eased back up to the peephole, and cursed himself. Fool! He'd done it again. He could only hope Fraser was too far off to see the flicker of movement. He should have more self-control by now. He shouldn't have let Fraser startle him. He kept himself at the peephole, determined to make no more mistakes.

The stallion tossed his head angrily. Fraser patted his neck without looking down and watched a moment more, then turned the horse again. They disappeared into the woods.

But Phin didn't believe it. Fraser suspected something. He wasn't done looking. The hoofbeats went off a ways, then stopped. For a while he heard nothing, or maybe a muffled stomp, far off. He watched, certain that Fraser had crept back to the edge of the woods. But he saw only water, sticks, trees—or was that a dark hat brim showing behind a tree trunk?

He stared at it a long time. It never moved. It was a branch.

But the earth rang as a horse stamped its foot somewhere deep in the trees. Fraser was still here. To his small list of advantages, Phin added the stallion's impatience, and the flies that tickled the slender black legs.

At last something moved; a man-size shadow among the tree trunks, going away. Another ruse, possibly. But after a time Phin heard hoofbeats, steadily receding.

Or were they?

No, they were above the dam. Fraser must believe he'd gone across.

He'd have to circle upstream to bypass the boggy ground. It would take time. Not much, with a horse of that quality, but some. When he reached the other shore, Phin and his scent-laden clothes would be upwind. Time to make another move.

Phin let himself into the pond. He was hot enough that it felt good for several seconds. He gulped water as he swam, cooling himself inside and out.

Abruptly he was too cold, aching with it, gasping. His legs cramped with knifelike pains. He struck out with his arms, reaching for the dam, and sank.

He bobbed up, choking and splashing, and caught at the dam barely in time. Coughing, sobbing, teeth clattering, he dragged himself onto warm dry sticks.

Too much—it was too much. Deep in his ice-cold body a match-flame of fury caught and burned. He wasn't an animal to be hunted like this.

He clenched his jaw to hold back the humiliating chatter. Shuddering, he retrieved his bundle and fumbled it open. Shirt, pants, then the coat, the wonderful coat. It felt warm as a coal stove after its time in the sun. He hugged it around him.

His feet were blue-white. He pulled his socks on, then the shoes, and finally checked his pockets. What did he have?

Matches. Knife.

Rope.

He stood for some minutes, looking at it, then glanced up at the sun. Riding high; edging toward afternoon, even? Best wait for dusk, if that was possible.

Crashing on the other side—the stallion was moving quickly. He'd crossed the brook already, was working his way through the brush toward the shore.

Phin walked back along the dam the way he'd come. He found the stallion's tracks, round and deep in the boggy ground, and followed them into the woods.

He nearly missed the scuffed place in the leaves; walked past it, and thought, Didn't I see something? and retraced his steps.

Faint tracks marked the spongy leaf litter. Phin followed down to the brook. Fraser would come back this way, since it had already proven passable.

Phin retreated upslope to dry footing. The horse would come slowly through brook and bog. When he reached dry land, he'd accelerate. Phin could see it, hear it, and carefully he chose his ground, where the stallion would be moving fast, but not too fast, where the trees grew close around the tracks, where there was only one way through, and where, in the exact place that he needed them, two trees stood close together on opposite sides of the little trail.

A faint shout from across the pond; Fraser trying his ploy again. He seemed very sure of Phin, seemed to know his quarry had not moved on.

Good.

Phin fumbled the rope out of his pocket with numb fingers. Now, how high?

If he got it wrong, this wouldn't work. Fraser would pass beneath the rope unscathed and the next minute have Phin by the collar.

Run the rope low and trip the stallion. That would work.

But Phin couldn't do it, not spill the beautiful animal in the dirt, risk injuring him. It was Fraser he must spill. The horse gave Fraser his advantage. Take that away and what would he be? Just a man, two-legged. And if Phin could catch the stallion . . .

He reached out with his arms, trying to recreate the

feeling of grooming the horse. About this high—and Fraser was a tall man. His shoulders framed the stallion's ears as he rode. So, put the rope—there. Clumsy with cold, he shinned up and made a knot, slid down, climbed the tree across the trail, rope in hand, and tied it fast.

When he'd finished, it seemed glaringly obvious, a thin dark line in the woods where nothing else was straight. Pathetically hopeful; the woods were wide, and there seemed no real reason for Fraser to take the same trail twice.

So maybe it wouldn't work. The only way to find out was to try.

He returned to the pond cautiously. He didn't want to be seen yet. On the other shore Fraser sat still as a statue in the saddle. The reins were loose. The bit dangled. Phin checked horse and rider against his mental image of them. About right, he thought; probably.

The horse shifted into the wind like a weather vane, nostrils flaring. When he stopped, he was pointing straight at Phin. Fraser reached into his saddlebags and took out a field glass. He aimed where the stallion aimed.

Phin made himself stay still, though the glass alarmed him. Fraser must have used it when he watched from the woods, must have seen something that made him pretty sure.

Fraser watched awhile, then dismounted, dropping the reins. The stallion lowered his head as if tethered to the ground, and Fraser started out along the dam.

In the middle, where Phin had hidden his clothes, he searched the dam itself, crouching and examining the sticks closely. Then he hunkered back and stared at the lodge for a long time.

Go on! Phin thought. Swim out! He would have liked to see that, and know exactly how cold Fraser was.

It didn't happen. Fraser walked back to his horse and got on. The stallion resumed his alert pose, and Fraser resumed scanning with the glass.

Phin let this continue as long as he dared, let the sun slip lower, let more time pass. Hunger grew in him. He felt empty as a starved wolf, and thirsty, too, which seemed ironic. Shivers chased each other up his spine, even in the heavy coat, and yet a strange excitement filled him. In this long cat-and-mouse game, finally he was the cat. He watched the stallion with a kind of craving—the swift slender legs, the ears nervous, flicking. If he could be quick enough when it happened—

Fraser's shoulders slumped. He was giving up. Phin stood.

The glass froze.

Phin took care not to move again. He must act in character. A fugitive under the gaze of his pursuer would be extremely careful, making only one or two mistakes.

Fraser watched intently. The minutes stretched, shadows lengthened and darkened. Short fall days; number four on Phin's list of advantages.

Finally, with a shrug—a theatrical shrug, perfectly visible across the pond—Fraser put away his glass and turned the stallion, riding off into the woods.

Phin listened hard. Yes! He was circling back the way he'd just come.

He was shaking, Phin noticed; not cold this time, excitement. He hurried toward his trap, toward where the stallion would run when Fraser was unseated.

Crashing above the dam as bog sucked at the horse's legs. A last floundering squelch, *rub-a-dub* of hooves on firm ground—

Then came the sound Phin had been waiting for. He was surprised at how small it was; no shout, no rattle of bones. Just a thud, and the stallion burst out of the trees, galloping straight toward him.

20
BEECHNUTS

The stallion's eyes bulged, white at the rims. Phin saw the swerve coming. The horse's momentum carried him closer but already, mid-stride, he was leaning away—

Phin lunged. His fingers brushed slick saddle leather. The stallion shied, melting under his touch, and it wouldn't work, Phin despaired—

The horse stepped on a flying rein, checked briefly, the rein snapped, and he exploded onward. In that brief pause Phin's hand closed on the saddle horn.

He was jerked off his feet, flying along half turned away from the horse. Trees rushed at him. He closed his eyes and twisted toward the stirrup, grabbing for it with his free hand, struggling to drag himself up, bashed by tree trunks, whipped by branches, thunder in his ears and his arm stretching—

His sweating hand started to slip.

It took forever, fraction by fraction. He was nothing but a hand, a failing grip. The rest of his struggles and flailing, the scratches, the buffets, felt distant, unimportant. Don't . . . let . . .

He lost hold suddenly; empty hand, empty air, and the ground came up under him hard.

Leaves under his cheek. Hoofbeats shaking the ground, smaller, farther, lighter, gone.

He opened his eyes. The world spun. He squeezed them shut and lay still.

He didn't know how long he lay there. Cold seeped up from the ground, even through the heavy wool coat, and that was what got him up finally.

The woods around him were completely unfamiliar. He had no idea how far the horse had carried him, or what to do next, which way to go.

Walk, then. Just walk.

His thoughts chased themselves, circling a hole in the center of his mind. He picked his way through the trees without really seeing them. His eyes couldn't seem to focus. Was it getting darker?

It was getting darker. The sun hid behind fast-moving clouds. A wind mixed streamers of cold air down from above. The wild gray sky matched Phin's mind.

He was in a very strange state. A small, detached part of him knew that, but he lacked the ability to examine it. He walked, not listening behind him anymore, feeling no fear and no urgency and in fact, no anything. Maybe this was all a story in a book. Maybe he wasn't really here.

Darker. Sun behind the hill.

He had no idea why he sat down. His knees just gave suddenly, and he collapsed on the leaves.

Keep going.

While it was still light.

He should . . .

He picked up a prickly nut, turned it in his fingers, pressed it hard. The sharp burrs hurt. He was here. He lifted the nut and tried to see it through his mental fog.

Nut.

Nut! Beechnut!

He looked around him on the ground. Another. A third. A scattering—

A squirrel on a branch above him scolded loudly.

A squirrel!

Phin got up on hands and knees and scrambled, grabbing nuts, putting them in his pockets. So tiny. So many. He stopped once, opened one with the Barlow knife, popped the sweet kernel into his mouth.

But over there a squirrel was working, getting some— he charged, chased it into the trees, dropped on his knees to hunt for more.

The sun was long down by the time he stopped. He couldn't see beechnuts anymore, could barely see the fallen limbs and twigs he must find to build a fire. It was getting cold. His hands felt raw with it.

He gathered sticks as quickly as he could. Not as many as up in the pinewoods. He had to roam far, though his back and hips and knees ached. Dark drew down rapidly. Returning from his last foray he almost missed his stick pile; stumbled into it by accident.

Better quit.

He wasted a match; it broke when he struck it. But the second flared, and after a few anxious moments feeding in tiny pieces of tinder, the fire took hold.

Phin sat close, stretching his hands to the blaze. He felt light-headed, and in spite of his frenzy about the nuts, not hungry.

That couldn't be true. He must be hungry. The woolly feeling in his head kept him from knowing things, kept the whole world distant. Out beyond him in the dark, he imagined Fraser reunited with his horse, but the figures were tiny, too far away to matter. He took out a handful of nuts—

Never mind nuts. Feed the fire. He shivered in his coat, crouching so close to the flames that the heavy wool started to smoke.

After a while he noticed that his sensible hands, with no urging from his mind, had been cracking beechnuts and supplying them to his mouth. He supposed they tasted good.

They seemed to.

Taste good.

Brr!

Dark now, black dark. No moon. He'd had the moon with him this whole trip. Now it was gone, too.

The last stick was long and thick. He fed it into the fire gradually, shoving it deeper each time the end burned off.

Curled up beside it.

Pillowed his head on the end.

Face warm, anyway.

❖ ❖ ❖ ❖ ❖

A touch on his cheek awoke him.

He sprang up, hitting and his hand struck something. His eyes popped open.

The sun glittered on a pillowy white landscape. Snow bent the branches and made caves and tunnels of the surrounding woods. The air smelled clean and moist.

In front of him the stallion backed away. He seemed gigantic, crisply black, with round smooth limbs and flowing mane. His eyes sparkled, his nostrils dilated, his tail dusted the snow, and his hard hooves trampled it.

He'd come close, the tracks showed, reached his nose to Phin's cheek. A gesture of friendship?

"Easy," Phin croaked. His throat hurt, but he was beginning to take in more. A long scratch marred the shining saddle leather. The reins were broken, and the bit still dangled.

Phin held out his hand. The stallion shied.

Something strange about the bridle. Phin's eyes felt prickly. He wasn't sure he was seeing right.

He reached in his pocket for some beechnuts, rattled them on his palm. At that the stallion's ears pricked and his dark eyes brightened. He minced forward, stretching his nose toward Phin's hand. Phin felt the familiar velvet muzzle, the strong lips squirming—

But barely opening. Hot breath on his hand, eagerness, but the horse only fumbled at the nuts.

Phin reached forward with his free hand. He took the dangling, broken rein stubs. The stallion bobbed his head lower, acknowledging capture, and Phin gasped.

The noseband was high on the bones of the stallion's face, and cruelly tight. It pinched the delicate skin into pleats and bulges. A small iron ratchet, like a latch, held it closed. The horse could open his lips but not his jaws, and he couldn't have eaten since Fraser had been swept from his back.

What kind of a man would do a thing like that?

Phin reached for the latch. The stallion tossed his head.

"Easy—" Phin suppressed his cough. Sudden sounds and movement had always disturbed this horse. Gently he scratched the velvet nose, rubbed upward and sideways. "Shh," he said. "Shh." A Dennis sound. They don't go by words, Dennis said. They go by what you do.

His fingers touched iron.

The latch was tight and took some strength to open, but it was well-made and worked smoothly. The leather band released. The stallion put his head down, shaking it, then shook his whole body, filling the woods with an enormous shuddering sound and the squeak of saddle leather.

Graciously he accepted a mouthful of beechnuts, delicately mindful of prickles.

Holding the reins as the horse crunched, Phin took his first real look at the morning. Five inches of wet snow had fallen. The clouds above were purple-gray like a pigeon's breast, and moving fast. It wouldn't snow anymore, he thought.

His throat ached badly. His feet were cold, but his hands must have been deep in the coat pockets all night, because they were fine. The heavy wool had kept his heat in, prevented it from melting the snow on top of him. He'd slept warm, really. He was all right. Just lost.

He looked at the horse, the saddle. The bridle with no reins. If only he had his rope—

He listened to the silent woods. Fraser was afoot now— they were both afoot. How far apart? Where was the pond? The road? The farm?

The stallion nudged his pocket. Phin brought out another handful of beechnuts and, offering them, stretched his arm, stepping toward the stirrup. The horse swung his rump away, unwilling for Phin to mount.

"Shh." It hurt less than speaking. "Shh."

As the horse took the nuts, Phin grabbed the saddle horn and stabbed his foot at the stirrup. The stallion whirled, the motion throwing Phin into the saddle. Snowy branches whapped his face. One hit hard, taking his cap. Snow went down his neck.

He ducked low, clinging to the horn with one hand and a twist of mane with the other. The horse wove through trees, his head low. Phin saw tracks, maybe horse tracks, but he was moving too quickly to focus.

Where was he being taken? The pond? The road? Somewhere else entirely? All Phin knew was the spring and power of the animal. He'd ridden mine mules and phlegmatic freighters who trudged and plodded and shuffled and jogged. This was something else entirely. Even the train seemed slow by comparison.

The trees thinned. The horse paused, and Phin raised his head.

In front of him stretched black water; a white-covered mound in the middle of it; a long, white-covered dam. A pair of ducks flew up and the water shuddered; rings spread.

The horse seemed to listen for some sound which didn't come. Now he went to the shore and drank. The rings spreading from his muzzle met the rings from the ducks, a pattern of shivering diamonds on green-black water.

With a sigh the stallion lifted his head. He gazed across the pond, then turned and looked toward the trees. With a little bob of his head he set off up the bank and into the woods, and at a familiar-seeming place, turned downhill.

Phin saw the dark line in the air, and a long shape in the snow beneath, unmoving. No, he thought. No, not dead. He never meant that. A fog filled his stomach.

Fraser lay face up, half flung against a tree. Snow was on him. One hand rested on his leg, gloved fingers loosely pointing toward the sky.

The stallion lowered his head. Phin gripped the saddle horn as dark muzzle brushed dark beard.

Fraser's eyes opened.

Phin vomited; just in time he leaned and missed soiling himself. The stallion shied, dumping him beside Fraser in the snow.

Fraser turned his eyes toward Phin. His tongue passed across his lower lip, moistening it.

"Grass," he said.

21
A MAN COMPLETE

"What?"

"Grassed me." Fraser's hand fell off his leg. His fingers splayed across the snow. "Grass."

"Snow," Phin said, and was surprised at the faint flash of amusement on Fraser's face. Oh. Grassed. The horse grassed me, people said; meaning, dumped me.

Phin stood up. He didn't know what to do or say, or think, or feel. He was aware of the broad silence around them, of being alone with Fraser; who lay where he had fallen, who hadn't moved all night; who was alive, but might not be much longer. Everything was suddenly much stranger. The air throbbed with it, and Phin was grateful when he thought of the next things to do. Brush his coat off. Kick some snow over the steaming patch of vomit.

As he did that, he looked covertly at Fraser. Something was far wrong with the man. He lay so still. Could his neck be broken?

But then he wouldn't be alive, would he?

He asked, "How bad are you?"

Fraser closed his eyes, and seemed to be assessing.

"Hard to say." He turned his eyes toward the stallion, vigorously gnawing tree bark. "Get your rope?"

Phin looked at it. It seemed impossibly high, though he'd climbed up and tied it only yesterday.

"Bad are you?" Fraser asked.

Phin shrugged.

"He can help." Fraser pointed at the stallion with his eyes.

Phin shook his head. "No reins." The way his throat felt, he grudged every word.

"Bring him," Fraser said.

Phin got the stallion and led him to his master, wondering at his own docility. There was no need to obey the helpless Fraser, but a thin clear oil seemed to flow through his head, and he did what he was told, waiting to see when he would come to himself again.

"Get on."

Phin moved toward the stirrup. The stallion started to swing away. "Ho," Fraser said softly.

The stallion froze. Phin crawled up into the saddle.

"Use your knees," Fraser said. He made a kissing sound to the horse, who moved forward. Phin pushed with his right knee, pointing the stallion toward one of the trees his rope was tied to. When he was under it, Fraser said, "Ho."

Phin could reach the rope easily now. He untied it and, winding as he went, pulled himself and the horse under him back toward the other tree.

He finished coiling the rope, and swung the stallion around. It was easy when you knew the trick of it. He looked down at Fraser. The man's eyes met his, making Phin think of Engelbreit.

With reason. Down there on the snow, Fraser looked up at a young enemy who suddenly had everything; a horse between his knees and a rope to make reins with; money in his pocket; a gun, doubtless, in the saddlebags. A man complete. Many a man had started life with less.

And what kind of a face did Fraser see? The last time Phin had looked in a mirror, he'd seen a lank and dreamy boy. He didn't think that boy was there now. What was there called forth fearlessness in a man like Fraser. That meant Phin was very dangerous indeed.

A strange exhilaration raced in his veins. He stroked the sleek arched neck in front of him. But his eyes stayed locked with Fraser's.

Who'd die if Phin left. Maybe he would anyway, but certainly he'd die left alone.

And Phin could ride away. He had that freedom; freedom to do wrong. He might pay for it later—probably he would—but at the moment nothing bound him.

He took in the awkward way Fraser lay, the shine of sweat on his skin. A pearly ray of sun penetrated the trees. Snow slid off a branch with a heavy sound; the leaves underneath gleamed wet and golden.

Had the horse stirred at that moment, had he taken a step in any direction, Phin might have nudged him in the ribs and ridden on. The balance quivered within him. It could tip either way.

The horse lowered his head, and heaved a sigh of boredom that rocked the saddle. The ordinary, human sound drew Fraser's gaze away from Phin's for a second, brought a flickering smile to his face.

"Aye, lad," he said. "Right enough."

Phin felt the pain in his throat again, and the shiver of fever on his skin. The exhilaration was still in him, and an easy-heartedness. Decisionless—after all, there was no decision to make—he stepped down from the saddle, thinking, A man complete. He hadn't been. He'd only thought so. But it became true the moment his foot touched ground.

He put the rope around the stallion's neck to hold him. "How do we do this?"

Fraser's eyes widened. He seemed to look through Phin at something far off. "Eat," he said after a bit. "Saddlebags."

Phin opened the nearest one. His old canvas jacket was stuffed in the top. That was what Fraser held under the stallion's nose, back by the abandoned house. It seemed small. He wondered if it had really fit him.

Under it was a leather pouch like an envelope, fastened with a thong, that contained about twenty pemmican cakes. They gave off a rich meat-and-berry smell.

Phin's stomach wrung as if it were eating itself. He snatched a cake and twisted off a bite. It was firm and resistant, rich with fat and fruit. He turned with one for Fraser.

"Him first."

"But—" Meat? The horse ate meat?

He held out a pemmican cake on the flat of his palm. The stallion blew a long warm breath over it, and with a pinched, peevish expression engulfed it. Phin got another cake for Fraser.

"Can you sit up?"

"I'd better. Be able to." Fraser braced his hands in the snow, and bent his knees in a slow vague way, as if unsure where they were. Beads of sweat popped out on his forehead. He pushed, turning pale, and inched slightly up the tree trunk. Phin stuffed his pemmican cake into his mouth and reached under the man's arm to help.

An iron hand siezed his wrist. Fraser's eyes glared into his. "Don't. Touch. Me!"

This close, Phin smelled blood, saw the dark crust on the breast of Fraser's coat. He nodded.

Fraser forced himself up another inch, a third, until he was more or less sitting. He was greenish, the lines deepcarved around his eyes. Phin put a pemmican cake into his slack hand. Fraser didn't want the food; Phin could see that. This was an effort of will and intelligence. Strength was needed; therefore eat.

Phin could already feel the strength himself. He took another cake. The stallion refused a second and gnawed bark above Fraser's head. Moving to stay close to the animal, Phin saw in the snow near Fraser's right hand a long and wickedly curved bowie knife.

Had he turned and ridden away, would he have gotten that between the shoulder blades?

He looked up from it, and met Fraser's amused eyes. "Nay," Fraser said, barely above a whisper. "I had other plans for it, lad."

Alone and starving in the snow; you could end it. One of the things you could do with a knife. Phin had kept himself from knowing that in his own dark hours.

"Cut a stick." Fraser made a circle with thumb and forefinger, showing Phin the diameter.

Phin handed him the horse's rope, picked up the bowie knife, and stepped away. There were branches all around and no need to go far, but he wanted to stand back from Fraser a moment. The smell of blood was heavy in his nostrils. He didn't understand how there could be blood, didn't understand Fraser's hurts.

He scooped a handful of snow and swallowed it. The cold eased his throat a little. He looked back at the man and horse beneath the tree. Fraser'd caught him in a way neither of them had expected. Or he had caught Fraser. However it worked out, they were in this together now. Phin squared his aching shoulders under the big coat, squeezed a hard lozenge of snow in his palm to suck, and cut a branch.

"Short," Fraser said when he brought it back. He spread his hand, showing how long. "In my mouth." Phin looked a question, and Fraser looked pain back at him. Phin understood; you bit a bullet, or a knife blade, or a stick, to keep from screaming.

Screaming would scare the horse.

The stick shook in his hand as he brought it to Fraser's mouth. Fraser had something to say first.

"Bring him. I'll stand. Put my . . . foot in the stirrup."

Now Fraser was ready. Phin put the stick between his teeth and he crunched it.

Phin took the stallion's rope and led him closer. Fraser reached up, his mouth straining around the stick, and began hand-over-handing up the stirrup leather. So slowly. Such a long gap between one hand reaching and the next reaching above it, feeling for the leather as if blindly. A sort of growl came out of Fraser. The stallion put his head high and pinned his ears, trampling the snow.

"Ho," Phin said. "Ho!" The horse quivered to stillness.

Fraser seized the horn and collapsed against the saddle. Sweat streamed into his beard. His breath whistled. The stallion's skin shuddered, and Phin stroked him. "Shh. Shh."

Finally Fraser lifted his head a quarter inch and nodded. Phin bent to his next task.

Fraser wore tall, slippery boots. His leg was heavy; Phin struggled to keep hold and lift it and stab his foot at the stirrup while the stallion minced up and down in place, his breath fluttering in his nostrils at this strangeness.

"Ho!" Phin gasped. Fraser's other leg collapsed for a moment, but his hands were clamped around the saddle horn and held him upright. Foot in stirrup now; a dangerous in-between moment should the stallion spook.

"Uh," Fraser said.

It was either a grunt of pain or a command. *Push*, probably. Phin put a shoulder to Fraser's backside and shoved with all his strength. Fraser slithered loosely into the saddle and fell forward on the stallion's neck.

His face had gone gray. He spit out the stick. It fell to the snow next to the stallion's front hooves, carrying a spray of blood dark as ripe berries.

"Tie me."

"Don't we need reins?"

Fraser just looked at him.

Phin loosed the rope from the stallion's neck, and wound it around Fraser and the saddle horn. He wasn't sure of the best way to do this, but the only help Fraser offered was a whispered "Ho," whenever the stallion moved.

When he had Fraser secured to the saddle, Phin went to the stallion's head and took the stubs of reins.

"No." Fraser's voice was hoarse. "He'll take us."

Where? Phin didn't ask. His throat hurt too much, and he'd find out soon enough.

"Grab his tail," Fraser said.

It wasn't an order Phin wanted to obey. The stallion stood high-headed, tense, and Phin remembered the kicks like pistol shots, the boards of the stall ringing.

"Tail," Fraser said.

Reluctantly Phin stepped behind the stallion and wrapped the luxuriant black hair around his hands and wrists. The powerful haunches were squarely in front of him. If the stallion kicked, he was dead.

"A'righ'?"

"Yes," Phin croaked.

Fraser made the kissing sound and the stallion started walking.

The sky was crisp and deeply blue. The snow sparkled with tiny lights—blue, green, red—and slid moistly off branches to show the bright fall leaves. Phin sweated in the cold fresh air. It all felt like fever—fever heat, fever images.

But it was real, and among the realest things were the stallion's fresh tracks in front of him; the deep triangular bite of the frog and the snow melted as well as compressed, as if the horse came hot from the underworld.

They traveled a long time. Phin's shoulders ached. His

wrists grew numb. Fraser was completely silent. Phin had no idea if he was conscious, or even alive. He was just a dark lump up there in the saddle, no help at all.

The stallion stopped. Phin stumbled into his haunches and he clamped his tail down, but didn't kick. Phin trudged up to his head to see what the matter was.

The graveyard. They had reached the back wall of the graveyard.

Before the stallion had jumped it. He couldn't now, with Fraser tied on like a sack of meal. Uphill Phin saw the farm buildings. He was walled away from them, would have to search for a barway—

A sound above him, not noticeably human, made him turn. Fraser's eyes were open. "Go," he whispered. "Gate. I'll jump."

Phin didn't have the strength to argue. He climbed over the wall and stumbled between snow-capped stones to the roadside gateway. There was no actual gate, just an opening, so he stood in the middle to block it.

Beyond the far wall, the stallion's head rose. The knife-shaped ears flattened, and he circled once. Then the hoof-beats came in a muffled drumming. The stallion cantered toward the wall with Fraser hunched over his shoulder. He soared across and landed skidding on the snow, snaking his head in triumph. Phin spread his arms wide as the stallion cantered toward him. "Ho," he croaked.

The horse dodged, blasting an excited snort. Fraser hung limp in the saddle. "Easy," Phin said. He reached for more nuts, but the coat pockets were empty.

The stallion stopped near Randal Collins's grave, turning to gaze at the wide pasture beyond the wall. He could so easily be away, carrying his helpless master with him.

Phin reached into his pants pockets. Tobacco. Horses and mules loved tobacco. He took out Dennis's knife and cut Jimmy's tobacco in half, releasing a richer scent. The stallion looked his way, nostrils flaring. His eyes brightened, and he came to Phin.

Phin gave him half the tobacco, then took the rein stubs and looked up at Fraser.

Unconcious, he seemed younger, his eyelashes dark and beaded with drops of melting snow. His slack hands still embraced the saddle horn. There was a fresh slick of blood on his coat. Wherever he'd meant for them to go, there was no instruction from him now.

Phin turned uphill, twisting his free hand into the stallion's mane for support. He walked toward the only sound in this whole bright morning, an irregular thump and crack, and came into the farmyard where Abby was splitting kindling.

22

DEAD-AND-ALIVE

Phin had been brought up not to startle someone splitting wood, but there was nothing he could do. Abby looked up, the hatchet kept swinging, and he closed his eyes, waiting for the horrible sound of her hitting herself.

Instead came a familiar uproar; his old friend Lucky by the front door, eyes bulging as if Phin and Fraser were his worst nightmare come to life.

When Phin looked away from the dog, he saw he needn't have worried about Abby. She had her hatchet well under control, cocked back like a weapon with the blade angled at him.

He opened his mouth and his voice failed. He tried

again, pushing out the only word he could think of.

"Sorry."

Anger flared in her eyes. "That's my *father's* coat!" Phin nodded.

"Abby!" a firm, ringing voice commanded. "Step back."

The grandmother stood in the open doorway. The rifle was too long and heavy for her, but it didn't matter. The barrel rested on the back of a kitchen chair, leveled at Phin's belt buckle.

Abby went to her side and turned to face Phin. The two women looked much alike: small, neat, and disconcertingly competent.

"You suppose he killed this man, too?" the grandmother asked. "Young fellow, I want you to know I can shoot a squirrel's eye out with this!"

Phin just nodded, just stared, and they stared back at him. Lucky filled the wordless stalemate with barks.

Abruptly something shoved Phin from behind and he stumbled. The short rein ends nearly pulled through his hand as the stallion turned. A throaty nicker came from uphill, and the mare hobbled around the corner of the barn.

"Oh for pete's sake! Abby, catch her! Put her in the barn!"

Abby went running, pulling off her apron. Lucky leaped and barked at her side. She twisted the apron into a rope as she ran, and intercepted the lame mare.

The stallion jerked his head, trying to follow. The bit still dangled below his throat and with only the loose noseband, Phin could barely hold him.

A whisper came from above; barely a whisper. Barely a breath. "Ho."

The stallion stilled, quivering. He struck out with one hard black hoof, just missing Phin, but didn't take another step.

Fraser lifted his head to look directly at the grandmother. He was a ghastly sight, corpse gray, with blood in his beard where he'd strained the stick hard against the corners of his mouth.

"We'd appreciate," he said. "Your help."

"So you're alive, are you?"

"Just," Fraser said, his voice a thread on the edge of breaking.

"Yesterday you said you were a lawman. Is the boy your prisoner?"

Abby came back in time to hear this. "Implied. Implied he was a lawman."

The grandmother turned to her. The rifle stayed steady,

pointed at Phin's middle. "They want help, Abby."

"They need it!"

" 'We,' he said. All of a sudden it's 'we.' But the boy's a murderer, we know that!"

Phin shook his head. Once it started shaking, it refused to stop. He stood helpless under their stares, trying to think what to say.

"*Accused* of murder," Abby said. "I don't think either one of them could murder a mouse right now. Do you?"

"A lot of men have walked up to a buck that looked dead and wished they hadn't. I don't know."

"Too long," Fraser said, "and I'll be gone. Bleeding."

The two exchanged a swift glance. The grandmother twitched the rifle upright and leaned it against the house. "Can you get him off the horse, boy, or are you as dead-and-alive as you look? Abby, what bed will we put him on?"

"I want him in the kitchen. Get blankets—" Abby whirled on Phin. "Can you get him down? What's your name? Why are you just standing there?"

He knew the answer to only one of those questions. "Phin. Chase."

"Chase," she said, and took a second in the crowded morning to really look at him. A smile warmed her eyes. "That's apt! Do you need help?"

He nodded. Fraser looked limp again, and yes, a trickle of blood ran down the stallion's dark shoulder.

"Untie him—no, bring him to the door first. Gran, will you *kill* that dog!"

In a few minutes everything was organized; Lucky locked in a back room, bedding brought to the kitchen, the stallion standing astride the front step and the grandmother at his head. Abby loosened the rope; "Is this *our* rope?" Fraser tipped slackly onto Phin's shoulders and braced arms.

The weight was too much. He couldn't really carry the man. He dragged him through the doorway and collapsed backward on the blankets with Fraser on top of him.

"Get up, get up! Take that horse away from Gran—put it in the other stall and get back here!"

Phin stumbled out the door. The grandmother was grimly hanging on. Phin took the reins and was towed toward the familiar barn.

He opened the door of the empty stall and maneuvered the stallion inside. The horse was dangerous now. Completely focused on the mare, he hardly seemed to notice Phin's presence. With clumsy fingers, Phin stripped off saddle and bridle and took himself away from the trampling hooves. The horses introduced themselves over the wall between the stalls, with sniffs, loud squeals from the mare, the ring of boards being struck by hard hooves. Phin hastened to bring armloads of hay.

Water? Were there buckets somewhere? And where was the well?

Water would have to wait.

He went back to the house. Warmth flowed out the open door.

They knelt on either side of Fraser. His coat was off, and Phin could see the dark crust of blood on his shirt. Tenderly the grandmother held a wet cloth to it. "I don't think we can get it off yet," she said to Abby. "Let me soak it a little more."

Abby looked up at Phin. "Close the door, for heaven's sake! Is this a knife wound or did you shoot him?"

"He fell."

"Just fell?"

"I—" Phin said. "With the rope . . . I don't know why there's blood." It made no sense, especially with the wound on the front of Fraser's body. If he'd landed on something, he'd be wounded in back, wouldn't he?

Abby got to her feet with a quick, graceful twist and went into the next room. After a moment she returned with a ceramic pitcher and basin, and a pile of clean white cloths over one arm. She put everything on the table. There was a mixing bowl on the table, too, a small bottle stuffed full of fuzzy purple flowers, a book with a worn cover.

Abby took the kettle from the stove and poured steaming water into the pitcher. She dipped her hands into a small crock. Phin smelled strong soap. Washing her hands, she looked keenly at him.

"Are you sick?"

He nodded.

"Go in there—" she pointed toward an open doorway off the kitchen. "Get the teapot and put in two scoops from the jar marked 'Boneset'—you *can* read?"

Phin laughed; not out loud, just a little breath. Engelbreit's house and *Leaves of Grass*; everything before and since, all in a flash not seen but felt, a twist of emotion in his body. He nodded.

"Two scoops of boneset, and fill the pot with hot water from the stove." Phin obeyed. "Then go out that door"— she pointed to one Phin hadn't noticed yet—"and pump me a bucket of water."

"The horses?" Phin croaked.

"What about—oh. There's a trough behind the barn— I'm amazed you don't know that! They'll have to be led out later. Now go!"

Phin went. The door opened to the back of the house, a yard with a pump. He worked the handle, more exhausted with every stroke, and turned with the full bucket. Abby stood in the doorway watching him as she dried her hands.

Did she think he'd run? Did she think he could?

He came toward her. She stood back to let him into the house, but her penetrating eyes stopped him.

"Why did you laugh?"

Phin's throat hurt too much for talking. Besides, he had no words. Here he was on this bright morning, being bossed by a girl who barely came up to his shoulder. She was in charge. Why her and not her grandmother? And where was the mother? He didn't know. He didn't know anything.

"Well, come on in, and close the door behind you. I don't want to touch anything. Now fill the kettle—thank you. And sit. Pour yourself a cup of tea and drink it right down—you won't like it! And then have another. Ready, Gran?"

Fraser groaned as his shirt peeled away from the wound. Phin saw a glimpse of milk-white torso tracked with red puckered scars, and a black oozing place low on his chest. He looked quickly away. Watch Abby. Sunlight through the window on her smooth clean hair. . . .

"That'll be a war wound," the grandmother said.

Abby bent close. She seemed cool, alert, thoughtful. "Look at that," she said to her grandmother. "Shrapnel, do you think?"

Fraser whispered something.

"Shell? Oh. Cannon shell. Sir—what's his name?" she asked Phin. "He told us yesterday, I suppose, but—"

"Fraser." And he'd have a first name, wouldn't he? David, maybe? Douglas?

"Mr. Fraser, I should take this out of your wound. The fall must have—oh, think of it, Gran! Like living with a knife inside you! May I try to take it out?"

Fraser's head barely moved on the bedclothes; a nod.

"Give him something to bite on, Gran—cloth is fine; he won't hurt himself. I wish Mummy would come back with the bag right now! I'll have to use my fingers."

The grandmother looked to be wringing her hands, but no, Phin saw, she was twisting a rag into a hard stick and now she put it between Fraser's teeth. "I wish she'd come, too," she said grimly. "That baby could have waited a day or two, seems to me!"

"Are you ready, Mr. Fraser?" Abby asked. "It's going to hurt. A lot."

It did, and it took a long time. That growl came out of

Fraser again. In the other room Lucky barked. A smell began to pervade the kitchen, of old blood and new blood, and around the edges of Fraser's growl a silence deepened. Whenever Phin glanced toward the mattress he saw Abby bent over, intent, her thumb and forefinger pinched on something and working it tensely. The thing was small and frighteningly tenacious.

He turned away, stared out the window at the snow melting in the warm sun, dripping off the eaves of the house. He tried to avoid hearing the small, wet sound within the room, not quite masked by Fraser's growl.

"There!" Abby held something up. It was smaller than Phin had expected, and it dripped—

"Abby, put your head down! Don't you dare faint on me till we've got this man bandaged!"

Abby turned abruptly from Fraser and sat bent over, hugging her knees. She held the shell fragment away from her skirt in red fingers. "Stupid," she said after a moment, her voice sounding slow and slurred. "I was doing so well and then—I *looked* at it. . . ." She swallowed audibly.

The grandmother knelt, pressing a cloth to the wound. For a moment there was no sound in the kitchen save Fraser's harsh breathing.

Unexpectedly, a sense of rightness dropped over Phin;

peace and piercing joy. The sun glinted off the teapot. A petal fell from one of the flowers onto the book. He gazed at it, feeling his heartbeat rock him slightly, feeling the warmth and his body relaxing in it.

The moment had edges. He knew it would end. But it went on a long time.

Abby stirred. With a guilty start, Phin poured himself a cup of tea. His hands felt pleasantly distant. Maybe they belonged to someone else.

He took a swig. It was horrible. Another gulp, three. He put the cup on the table, reached toward the pot again, and then, no, he thought he'd just put his head down on his arm, arm of the worn old military coat. *Essays*, Emerson, said the gold letters on the spine of the book. In a second he'd pick it up, but just now he'd close his eyes. . . .

23

MATCH LIGHT

There were dreams. A hand laid on his forehead as his mother used to, checking for fever. Far-off neighing. Cooking smells.

A voice said, "Not in our rooms! Not till we know."

Later he woke up someplace else.

No, same place, but on the floor, looking up. A curtain beside him. No, a skirt. In a chair. The grandmother, knitting, looking grimly past Phin at something beyond him.

He wanted to look, too, but it was too much effort to lift his head. He lay staring at the skirt, the stove, sunshine through the legs of chairs and table. There was a sound behind him, regular, harsh. Fraser, he decided after a bit. Breathing. He closed his eyes again.

"I don't know what to do," a voice said. Maybe it was later. "If I take her out, he'll jump the door, and I don't dare touch *him*. But they need water."

"You," another voice said. "Boy!"

"Phin. His name is Phin."

Phin opened his eyes again. Abby and her grandmother looked down at him.

"Could you help me take them to water?"

Them.

The horses.

Phin struggled up on his elbows. His head felt stuffed with hot wool. His eyes wouldn't fully open, and he ached everywhere. When he tried to speak, his voice choked off. He nodded, and then faced the prospect of getting up.

"I wouldn't ask if I didn't need to." Abby reached down a hand. Phin took it. A firm grip on his elbow boosted him to his feet.

The bedding was next to the stove now. He didn't know how he'd gotten there, beside Fraser.

Who looked up at him. His eyes shone like pools of mercury. Phin had seen that shine in the eyes of four people. Three were now dead.

"How lame is the mare?" Fraser sounded weak, but

surprisingly rational. "Can she go far?"

"She bowed a tendon three weeks ago," Abby said. "She can hardly hobble."

"Turn them loose. If you don't mind a foal next summer." He closed his eyes. In the shadow beside the stove, his lids looked purple. Abby bit her lips, looking at him. Then she turned away.

"I can probably let them loose myself."

Phin didn't bother to shake his head. He followed her out into the sunny afternoon. The air chased shivers over his skin, even inside the heavy coat.

The mare stood in the farthest corner of her stall, ears back scornfully. The stallion leaned over the dividing wall at her. He looked magnificent, his eyes brilliant, his neck arched. He didn't so much as flick an ear at Phin and Abby.

"He'd better not hurt her!" Abby said. Phin just pointed at the mare's door.

Abby looked at him soberly. "Me first, then you?"

Phin nodded.

"I'll lead her outside, right? So we aren't trapped in here with them?"

Hurry, Phin mouthed.

Abby opened the mare's door and looped a strap over her neck. The mare followed her, and the stallion shoved against the door of his stall. Then—was this more fever?—he reared slowly, like a dog sitting up for a crust of bread, and looked over the half-door, judging the distance to the floor.

"Go!" Phin croaked. Abby hauled the mare out the doorway and sprang aside.

"All right!" she called.

Phin threw open the stall door. The stallion's hooves drummed briefly on the barn floor and then came an enormous squeal. Phin hurried outside.

The stallion was beautiful with Fraser riding him, and beautiful in a stall. Now, as he danced courteously beside the limping mare, pointing his ears at her, stretching his neck to venture a sniff at her flank, he was more than beautiful. The mare threatened him with a hind foot. He curved away, and back to her, and Phin shook his head. He had ridden that horse? It didn't seem possible.

"We'd better shut the door so they don't get into the oats," Abby said. "Can you help?"

The door was a wide one, mounted on an iron roller. Abby pushed and Phin pulled feebly, and they got it closed.

"Now back by the stove. You're going to have another cup of tea and you're going to sleep some more."

And he did.

❖ ❖ ❖ ❖ ❖

When he woke again it was dark, inside and out. A candle on the table barely illuminated part of the kitchen. The grandmother sat in a rocking chair, a blanket wrapped around her. The shine of her eyes told Phin she was watching them.

Phin sat up. He still ached, but more distantly, and he didn't feel stronger so much as lighter. It was easy to sit up because he weighed nothing.

The grandmother pressed her finger to her lips. The chair creaked as she got out of it, bringing him a cup.

"Abby says you're to drink this."

"I—need to go out first."

"Go, then. Shh."

Phin glanced at the shape beside him on the blankets. Fraser lay staring at the ceiling, chewing his lower lip. His eyes still had that over-brilliant glitter, but as Phin rose they turned his way, clear and lucid. Phin felt a jump of alarm, which he hoped didn't show. He gave Fraser a little nod and slipped out the door.

The moon was up. Phin followed the trail of footprints to the outhouse. Around the corner of the barn he heard crunching and looked uphill. Two horse shapes bowed their heads and pawed the snow. A cow shape stood watching.

The beauty stopped Phin. Weak and clearheaded, he

took in the world around him. White pastures stretched up the hill. The color of the leaves was visible in the moonlight; their spicy scent was present in every breath, cooled and freshened by snow.

He walked up toward the animals. The mare whooshed her breath at him. The stallion touched his nose to hers. Phin turned his back, did what he'd come out for. After a moment he felt a nudge on his arm.

He stroked the stallion's face, his flowing forelock, the hollows above his eyes. The high neck curved around him. The stallion pushed at the pocket of this coat—

—that didn't belong to Phin. Horse that didn't belong to him; farm that didn't belong to him, under a moon that belonged to no one. Nothing belonged to Phin Chase and he felt a wild joy rising; because of that, or anyway. He was alive. Fraser was alive and the horses and cow and the women, the trees—all alive. He wanted to sing, or strike one of those long keening notes on a fiddle; failing that, to run his hand along the neck of a beautiful horse seemed a kind of singing.

The stallion turned away from the empty pocket with a faint sigh. Phin searched his pants for the last nugget of tobacco. His hands found knife, wooden matchbox; Plume's money.

He looked down at the dimly lit kitchen window. As he watched, it was blocked briefly; the grandmother maybe, peering out. Maybe Fraser had asked her to. He was awake in there, aware. Injured though he was, he hadn't forgotten his mission, and there was no guarantee as to what would happen next. Phin might get sicker, fall into Fraser's power. He might waken in handcuffs—

Or it might all go another way entirely. But whatever Fraser was—lawman, Pinkerton agent, some higher-up in the Sleepers, even; that was remotely possible—Phin knew there was one thing he had to do.

His fingers, by now, knew the difference between the money and the letter or list, whatever it was. He took it out of his pocket. Gripping it in his teeth, he pulled off the tight cover of the box and shook out a match, struck it on one of the stone gateposts and held it near the paper.

Last chance; for power, if this was power. To bargain, if Fraser wanted it.

Last chance to read the thing.

Worth the lives of six men.

Maybe they were mine supervisors, like Engelbreit. Maybe they were Sleepers, killers like Plume; or heroes fighting for their people; or both. It didn't matter. Whoever they were, the power that paper held over them didn't belong to Phin or Plume. It didn't belong to Fraser either.

Phin touched the flame to the corner of the paper and dropped the match hissing in the snow. The bright, pure flame blossomed up the sheet, making the handwriting stand out briefly black and stark. The glow warmed his face.

Then the heat reached his fingers. He let the paper fall. It curled, and the flames sank to a tracery of embers. Phin crouched and felt where he'd last seen it. There was nothing left.

24
BLOODHOUND

The kitchen seemed small when Phin went back in, the warmth stifling. Fraser lay with his face turned toward the door. His eyes followed Phin across the room. Phin stretched his hands to the stove. A smear of soot on one finger; he rubbed it off.

The old woman rose and poured him a cup of tea— different than before, less bitter. The first swallow hurt, the second hurt less, and the third was easy and normal.

"He's to drink, too," she said. "Can you help him? I don't get down easy this time of night."

Phin knelt beside Fraser. He smelled match sulphur

on himself. Fraser might notice, but what could he do about it?

He raised Fraser's head gently from the pillow and tipped the tea into him. Fraser swallowed obediently a few times, then closed his lips and turned his head away.

"It's Abby's judgment you may die of this," the grandmother said in a small, dry voice. "We're trying to give you every chance."

Fraser nodded, so small a movement that Phin might only have imagined it. His lips parted again. Phin trickled in the tea, waiting while Fraser swallowed. The man's skin shone with sweat. "I—I'm sorry—"

"You've no killed me yet, lad." Fraser closed his eyes. Phin sat back, handing the cup to the grandmother.

"Scotch, is he?" she asked.

"He's Scottish," said Fraser, voice light and buzzy as a fly at a windowpane. "I'll tell you about him, so if he dies, you'll know."

"Should you talk?"

"It's talk or weep, ma'am. Let me talk. What do I call you?"

"You call me Mrs. Collins until my daughter-in-law comes home. Then you'll call me Grandma Collins, if I decide to let you."

"Your daughter-in-law. I've seen her . . . in Washington? In the war?"

"She went to nurse my son. She arrived too late."

"Aye, she had that look . . . like a blind angel."

"Don't talk in that novelish way to me." Tears glistened on the old woman's lower lids.

"Gran?" Abby stood in the kitchen doorway.

Grandma Collins lifted her chin, seemed to drain the tears back into herself. "Did we wake you?"

Abby shrugged. "Keep talking. I'll poach some eggs." She lit a second candle.

Fraser lay staring at the ceiling, biting his lower lip. His eyes squeezed shut, and then slowly opened. "Is he all right, lad?"

He? Oh. The horse. "Yes," Phin said, expecting to croak. But his voice came almost normally. What was in that tea?

"He can't eat. The day and night—he won't have eaten. Cut it off—if he comes back—I'll cut it off. But hurry, lad, there's no much time."

The cruel noseband; that was what Fraser was talking about. That's what the knife had been for. "It's off," Phin said. "He's fine."

"What's he talking about?" Abby asked in a low voice.

"The horse is . . . like a bloodhound," Phin said. "It's how he followed me. He takes the bit out—and the noseband's very tight, I don't know why—and it tracks just like a dog."

"Stops him eating," Fraser said. "He'll no work if he can eat."

"And the horse tracked you?" Abby caught her grandmother's eye. They looked at each other for a long moment. Wood popped inside the stove and water gently bubbled in a pan. Both women glanced toward the rifle in the corner.

Phin felt the fear in the room. They'd forgotten to be frightened; they'd been too busy. Now he'd reminded them. Ducking his head, he crossed to the blankets and sat down, making himself small and unthreatening. In a back room Lucky whined.

"Speaking of dogs!" Abby said brightly. She left the kitchen. A door opened deeper in the house, and she spoke Lucky's name.

Phin braced for the barks. But Lucky came meekly into the room, tail wagging low. He sniffed Phin thoroughly, eyebrows working, gave Fraser a brief inspection, then flopped on the blankets and offered Phin his belly for scratching. Abby and her grandmother looked ruefully at each other. The grandmother said, "How much judgment do you think this animal has, Abby?"

Abby laughed. "You were the one who said, *'They know!'* when he bit the doctor. You've passed a test of sorts, Mr. Chase!"

"Phin Chase," Fraser said, drawing all their eyes. "Phin Chase was in the wrong place—say Phineas, so the line comes right." He raised his voice, thin and reedy in song. "Oh-h-h, Phineas Chase was in the wrong place, At Engelbreit's table one day—" He broke off with a grimace. "Hurt some ribs, too," he added conversationally.

Abby and her grandmother exchanged sober looks. Abby moved the kettle to a hotter place on the stovetop, and took her candle into the pantry.

She came back with another teapot and poured in boiling water. The kitchen filled with a pungent scent that reminded Phin of horse linament. She scraped butter on a slice of toast, put an egg on top, and said to Phin, "Will you come to the table?"

He got up. He still had the coat on. He should take it off, stop reminding them he was a thief. But he felt so warm—too warm, and that seemed right. Sweat out the sickness. He took a chair and picked up fork and knife, though he wanted to ignore the civilized utensils and cram the food in with his hands. The first mouthful brought tears to his eyes.

"The horse," Fraser said from the floor. "He's all right, lad?"

"A' righ'," Phin said, muffled.

The grandmother said, "I remember Grampa saying—and this goes back a ways!—that there were men in England that called their horses in by smell. And it was herbs, too, Abby. I wish I knew what. They'd rub a little on themselves—say, where the vein jumps in the neck—and they'd go stand in just the right place for the breeze to take it. By and by the horses would come in, and they'd catch them and go to work."

"Caught him like that," Fraser said.

It jolted Phin, how he followed the talk. He seemed to drop in and out of delirium. Was that real? With Fraser you always had to wonder.

He went on, stronger seeming, about working a wild bunch with the Cheyenne. They'd driven the horses with their man smell, with the horses' fear of it—miles, without ever laying eyes on them until they were in the trap.

And Fraser had wondered: If men could catch horses by smell, couldn't horses catch men? Could you train one to? And he'd done it.

"Now who needs men caught? Where's the action? For real scope—go to Allan Pinkerton."

"And you did?" Abby asked.

"Aye. That's what I did."

Phin swabbed the last trace of egg off his plate with the last corner of bread. So Fraser was a Pinkerton agent. He felt he'd always known that.

"The Pinkerton Detective Agency," the grandmother said. "I always think of Emerson—"

"Oh," Phin said, without thinking. "The transparent eyeball!"

The room went quiet. Everyone was looking at him.

25

THE TRANSPARENT EYE

The old woman asked, "What do you know about the transparent eyeball, boy?"

"Phin," Abby said.

"It's—it's in 'Nature,'" Phin said. "He's talking about the woods—"

"And he turns into an eyeball," Fraser said. Abby laughed.

"It wasn't written to be amusing," her grandmother said. "Maybe you can tell me what it's about, b—young man."

"I—I can quote it." Phin pinched the fallen petals on the table into little heaps. "He's talking about how nature . . . lifts you up, and he says—'I become a transparent eyeball; I am nothing; I see all; the currents of the

Universal Being circulate through me; I am part or parcel of God.'"

"Aye," Fraser said. His delirium, or whatever that had been, seemed suddenly cooled. "'Currents of the Universal Being.' Aye."

The quiet in the room grew deeper, more emphasized than broken by the crack of wood in the stove.

"Anyway," Phin finished lamely. "I think Pinkerton's eye is different."

"I think so, too," the grandmother said, with a grim smile. "Young man, we've had one account of you. Now I'd like yours. A boy from a coal patch—we were told you'd shot a man. Who are you? How do you know Emerson?"

It felt like a boulder rolled off Phin's heart. After the tumult of the last few days, to have the most pressing question be about a book . . .

"I read the essays to my mother while she washed clothes. At Murray's Tavern, where I was raised."

He told of his father, conscripted and marched away to war; his mother moving to Murray's and how she kept him out of the mines; the washtub readings. How, when Phin was old enough to understand that people disapproved, she told him, "'My life is for itself, and not for a spectacle,'" quoting Emerson again. "I know what's right for me," she went on in her own words, "and I'm willing to trust my judgment."

Then she laughed and said, "We're a pair of spectacles, Phinny!" Phin's voice thickened at that, but he pushed on. Her death, John Engelbreit and his books, and the sunny morning when Ned Plume walked up the path with a pistol in his hand.

And the rest; a sketch of it, anyway. He didn't mention Margaret or the wallet, and he felt Fraser watching, waiting for more.

"And you ran?" Abby said. "I don't understand. I mean—at that moment, of course, but couldn't you go to the constable?"

Fraser stirred. "Ladies," he said. His voice came deeper, stronger; alarmingly so. "You've heard of the Molly Maguires?"

The women exchanged a quick look.

"That's what Plume is. A Molly gunman—Sleepers, they call them in Bittsville, an old name. It's a secret society . . . and in coal country, anyone who fires an Irishman's in danger from them. As are the Welsh miners. As are the English. As are half their fellow Irish, truth be told. We don't know who they are, half of 'em . . . but for sure, the constable's a Sleeper.

"Now the owners—they're fed up. Ready to hang some Irish, set an example. They think Phin killed their man Engelbreit, and . . . they won't wait for explanations. Sleepers—they've got other reasons for wanting him. Lad's between a rock and a hard place. He did right to run."

Abby moved from her place by the stove, bringing the candle with her. As she set it on the table, it cast a brighter light on Fraser's face. "But you know he's innocent," she said. "Did you always know?"

Fraser turned his head on the pillow. "What makes you say that?"

"Phineas Chase was in the wrong place, you said. In your song."

"What song would that be?"

The question rang false and over-theatrical; false as Fraser's lies in the freight car. Abby looked at her grandmother, communicating something without words.

The old woman said, "Talks like a novel. I know. You're not very good at this, are you?" she said to Fraser.

His eyes widened. He looked from one to the other, between amusement and alarm. "Perhaps not!"

"Why did you chase Phin?" Abby asked. "What are you up to?"

They were entirely on his side, Phin realized. They

simply believed him, a ragged boy who'd stolen from them. Until he quoted from "Nature" it could have gone either way, but now he belonged. He was their kind.

Fraser lay still in his blankets. They'd come to the nub of things.

"My motives are—mixed," he said, "and maybe you're right. Maybe I'm not very good at this. Engelbreit—I didn't see that coming. I came on the scene—they tried their story on me—and I thought . . . get you first. So I took the jacket—that I am good at, ma'am—and we trailed you. Lost you on the hill—behind the houses—but there you were. Back at the barn.

"Thought I'd get you off somewhere. Get your story. That had to be done in secret, so I waited my chance—and what do I find? That you're a bit of a rascal yourself, Phin Chase. Forked Plume's wallet. *Plume's!*"

He smiled faintly, shaking his head, and Phin felt himself turn color. He looked away, smoothing his face. Fraser didn't know Margaret's role. Plume hadn't told that part of things, despite the rage that made him careless of other secrets.

Fraser said, "It emerged—you had a paper on you, of interest to me. Extreme interest. You got on the train— what a chance that was! But along comes Plume, drunk as a lord—and off we all go. When he went under—I could have had you then, lad. But I drove you farther. By then . . . I wanted to get away myself.

"You left the train. I followed, but you shook me off again." He grinned, showing his teeth. "My intentions being unbeknownst to you."

"Why did you want to get away?" Abby asked.

"Because I know what's going to happen."

He let that hang and Phin thought, Novelish, and none of them obliged him by asking "What?"

"There's an almighty cave-in coming," Fraser said. "All over coal country. Pinkerton's got us everywhere, picking up scraps to braid into hangman's rope."

"And have you lost your taste for that employment?" Grandma Collins asked dryly.

"I have," Fraser answered. "I don't hold with the Sleeper killings, but they're trying to help their people. And yet"—he looked Phin in the eye—"with all my fine scruples, lad, don't be assuming I'll help you."

"You have to help!" Abby said.

"I've lived a hard life, miss, and I've found there's few things a man has to do. We have a wide latitude."

Phin knew that. He'd considered leaving Fraser in the snow to die, been free to do that. He would have harmed himself greatly, but that wasn't what stopped him.

"Do I need your help?" he asked Fraser.

"Aye. If I bring you in, you're a witness. If I don't—you're a wanted killer with Pinkerton on your trail."

"I could disappear," Phin said. "Tell Pinkerton I'm dead."

Fraser shook his head. "That won't help either of us. Once Pinkerton's on the trail, he never gives up. He'll open a grave with his own hands to be sure the right man's in it."

Phin pinched the bridge of his nose, trying to think. Run? Spend the rest of his life a murder suspect? Or go back to testify, and be killed by the Sleepers . . .

"There's another way," Fraser said. "You took a paper off Plume. There's a list. Give me that. If it's as important as he thinks—that nets me six big fish, and you don't matter at all, lad."

"I thought you were through braiding hangman's rope!" Abby said scornfully.

"I don't know what I am and that's straight, or as straight as I know how to be after all this time. But I took the job and I'll carry it through."

Phin stood up. That said it all, really. He could stand. Fraser couldn't. He reached deep in his pocket and brought out the roll of bills, and bending, fanned them before Fraser's eyes. "This is all I have from Plume."

Two spots of red blazed on Fraser's cheekbones. His eyes bored into Phin's. "There was no paper?"

Phin shrugged.

"Come, lad, where is it?" He managed to sound threatening, even flat on his back. "Did you read it, at least?"

Phin shook his head. "Decided I'd—rather not. I burned it."

Fraser's nostrils flared. "Just now? Did I smell it?"

Phin nodded.

Fraser's face twisted for a moment, in intense frustration, and he made a small motion under the blankets, as if slamming his fist.

Then he smiled a crooked, resigned smile, and closed his eyes. "So be it. Consider yourself . . . my prisoner. I'll . . . keep you safe. Better pray I live."

Phin tried to answer, but his throat had closed up again. He poured himself more tea as Fraser said,

"Maybe you'll no have . . . to testify. If they spring the trap before Plume—"

His voice sliced off. His eyes flew open, staring at the ceiling. "Lad, I'm sorry," he said after a minute. "I was forgetting. Plume's here. At the doctor's. He saw you get off. Soon as he's able . . . he'll be looking."

26
ON THE WAY

Phin looked quickly toward the window. It was gray now, not glossy black. Dawn coming.

"He'll not likely get . . . wind of you here," Fraser whispered. A look passed between Abby and her grandmother.

"Will he?" Phin asked.

"Alma's out birthing a baby," Grandma Collins said. "We told the father about you two when he came to fetch her."

"And once the Wright girls visit the Brinkleys, that's the whole village told!" Abby said tartly.

"But not tonight." Grandma Collins pinched the bridge of her nose. "Surely we could all sleep, and think this through in the morning?" She looked older, frail and exhausted. Abby gave her a worried look, and then glanced at Fraser, lying with his eyes closed.

"I . . . think so," she said, putting her hand to her forehead. "She only went this morning. I don't see how he could have found out yet. Call us," she told Phin earnestly, looking straight into his face. "If you feel worse, or he does—don't hesitate. All right?"

And they left the kitchen, taking Lucky with them.

Phin looked at the gun in the corner. He'd never shot a gun, never even loaded one. Murray'd steered him clear of weapons. "Learn to use it or don't pick it up," he'd said. "Bluffing's the quick way to get killed." But it was none of his business to teach tavern help to shoot, even if Phin had wanted to know.

He got up and went to the window. The yard was peaceful, empty. He stepped to the back door. The hillside stretched below him, barely sensed. Not even an owl disturbed the quiet, but if he listened hard he could hear, almost, the clink of glasses on a bar, the scraping of a fiddle.

He was exhausted, and his throat was starting to hurt again. He stretched out on the blanket and wrapped the coat around him. From where he lay he could see stove, table, book, gun. He had to stare hard to keep them all in place. If he lost focus for even a moment, they whirled around the room—table upended, book flying, stove—

No. He blinked, hard, to drive away the image of Engelbreit calm-eyed against the stove. But he always came back.

Plume walked through the open door, slim and broad-shouldered, rimmed with sunlight, and the gun exploded—

No. Phin was *here*, on this floor, in the dark. Fraser breathed beside him and the door was shut—

—and the next moment Plume said, light and rueful as a man refusing an olive, "This one I can't do."

It happened too many times and finally, angrily, Phin sat up—

—to find sunlight splashed bright across the kitchen floor and the cow lowing resentfully. Behind him Fraser breathed deep and slow.

Abby stumbled through the kitchen, rubbing her eyes. She glanced toward Phin and Fraser as if her mind wasn't working yet, got her pail, and went to the door. She opened it, the light threw her shadow long on the floor, and Phin found himself on his feet, heart pounding.

The shadow had skirts, not a hat and gun. He followed her outside.

The sun was mid-morning high in a soft blue sky. A creamy haze floated above the trees downhill.

Abby went toward the barn, stopping abruptly at the

closed door. "Here." Phin shrugged out of the coat, and helped her put it on. Together they walked to where the cow tugged at her tether. Phin scratched the annoyed animal while Abby knelt, arranging the skirts of the coat under her to keep her dress dry. She rested her cheek against the smooth swelling side. Milk hissed rhythmically into the pail and Abby closed her eyes.

Sorry, Phin wanted to say. *Sorry for the trouble*. He looked off downhill. "How far is town?" he asked.

"Four miles. That way." Abby pointed with her chin.

Four miles was nothing.

"He might not hear about you," Abby said. "Maybe he'll go away."

Plume looked up at Phin from the pile of hay with hot, hard eyes.

"Or can't you hide up on the hill? We'll say we never saw you again."

Phin imagined it, and it made sense. With a supply of food and a coat, maybe a blanket, he could live up there awhile, watch the farm—

But his imaginings took him farther. Plume coming, not believing the story he was told; how would he force the truth out of them, or out of Fraser, helpless on the floor—

"If he comes, it's too late."

"Then we'll hold him off. Gran can shoot—almost as well as she claims!—and Fraser's got at least one gun—"

"He does?"

"A derringer, in his sleeve. You didn't know? There's a knife, too."

"I saw that." Phin turned to look at the house. From below as he'd fled it had looked like a fortress. Now it seemed gentle and domestic, a broad-beamed old lady dressed in gray. It had seen its pig killings and the beheading of chickens for Sunday dinners, its family deaths in back bedrooms. It had never seen anything like Plume.

He glanced down the farm road. No one was coming.

Abby stood up and looked, too. "I never used to think about what a lonely place this is."

"Sorry," Phin said, and she looked up at him with a rueful smile.

"Sorry butters no parsnips. Why don't you move this cow for me, and then come on inside."

The kitchen was warm. The stove crackled with life, the teakettle crooned, and Grandma Collins stood stirring a pot of oatmeal. In the pantry Abby was setting the milk to cool. In spite of everything, Phin felt his spirits lift. He looked to Fraser, expecting to see the strength he'd shown last night. But Fraser lay flat in his blankets, eyes wide and dull in a yellowish face.

"How are you?" Phin asked.

The words seemed to reach Fraser slowly. He licked his lips. "Bad."

Abby bent and put her hand on Fraser's brow. She looked at her grandmother. Grandma Collins shook her head slightly, lips pressed together. "I know who I want to see come through that door."

"Maybe this afternoon," Abby said. "All those girls—someone should be old enough to help by now."

Phin expected they would do something for Fraser. Instead Abby asked him to put a kettle of water on the stove. Then the three of them sat down to breakfast; oatmeal, with cream and maple sugar, and strong hot tea. While they ate, the kettle started steaming. When they were done, Phin set it beside Fraser's blankets, and Abby knelt to examine the wound.

She loosened the bandage. A smell was released, and Phin found he needed to step outside.

He looked down the road, and listened. He collected eggs, imagining once or twice that he recognized the hen that had been his intended victim. He moved and filled the cow's water tub.

Then he walked up to the field, telling himself he was checking on the horses. There was nothing to check. They were completely self-sufficient. Even the lame mare evaded Phin easily.

But when he turned to look downhill, the roofs were small, and he saw how far away from the house he was already. He could just keep going—

The stallion nudged his shoulder. Phin ran his hand along the dark arched neck. He had no rope, but he could go down and get one, get the bridle—

The horse pricked his ears toward the road. Phin looked, too. Did the stallion smell something? If so, he dismissed it; dismissed Phin, too, turning abruptly from the hands that produced no tobacco or beechnuts, not even a pemmican cake. Phin had to smile. He went back to the house.

Fraser had been rebandaged. He lay as still as a fallen leaf, and Abby sat beside him, watching soberly. "Mr. Fraser," she said after a while. "You've got to take hold."

"Should we go for the doctor?" Phin asked.

"If you want to kill him!" Phin flinched. "Sorry, but he's not a good doctor. Anyway, you can't go. Plume is there."

"He could go for Alma," Grandma Collins said.

Abby considered that. "No," she said finally. "Mummy'll

come as soon as it's right to leave. We can't call her away if the baby needs her."

"Then it's up to us."

"And him."

They looked down at Fraser. He was conscious, clearly. His jaw was tightly clamped, and once in a while he licked his dry lips.

Grandma Collins picked up the book from the table, and began to page through it thoughtfully. "You two go away for a while. This is old people's work."

Abby led Phin off to the parlor. It had a look of lost prosperity: worn velvet chairs, a scuffed carpet, and books on shelves, on tables, piled against the wall. "It's how people pay us, sometimes," Abby said, seeing Phin's amazement. "If we lived nearer town, I'd open a library."

Phin sat in a stout, gentlemanly chair, glancing sideways at the nearest stack of books. Dickens's name repeated on seven spines. He hadn't read any of them; he wished he wanted to now. He got up and crossed to the window, looking out at the yard. The only things moving were the hens.

"You're making me nervous," Abby said. "You beat Fraser. Did you notice that? You're someone to be reckoned with—but you're as jumpy as a cat on wash day!"

Phin turned away from the sunny scene. "You don't . . . have a cat," he managed.

"She disappeared this spring. I'll insist on being paid in kittens, next time I see a likely one."

The room was abruptly shadowed. Phin turned. Only a cloud, gusting across the face of the sun.

"Please," Abby said. "Sit down. Lucky will let us know if someone comes."

Phin sat. He didn't know what to say. Abby didn't seem to, either. Grandma Collins's voice reached them, a long murmur without defined words.

"Do you remember your father?" Abby asked suddenly.

Phin shook his head. But clearly she wanted talk, and he found himself telling her about Murray, and Dennis.

"So you had fathers, in a way. I didn't—only Emerson!"

"He was like my uncle," Phin said. "Like the one in Ireland. I mean—I never met *him* either." He went to the window again.

"This is absurd!" Abby got up, too. "Let's go see how he's doing."

"Do you think—"

"I don't know. Life flares up and down. You can't tell when it's guttering like this. He might very well live."

Phin took this to mean *He probably won't*. He pressed his

head against the cool windowpane. If Fraser died he'd have to keep running. Maybe he should be running now, because how much help could the man be flat on his back?

Lucky barked outside and Phin heard hoofbeats. He drew back from the window, heart pounding. A buggy—

"Oh, thank goodness!" Abby rushed out of the room. A moment later Phin recognized the horse as the one he'd seen from the graveyard.

Abby's mother got wearily down and came toward the house carrying a basket and carpetbag. An even wearier man followed her with a bushel crate. Phin retraced his steps through the unfamiliar house, reaching the kitchen by one door as Abby's mother entered by another.

She paused just inside, sniffing the air sharply, and weariness seemed to fall away from her. "What's wrong?" she asked, looking around. Then she swept across the kitchen and dropped on her knees beside Fraser, bag and basket forgotten on her arms. "What happened?"

Her voice was soft and breathy. Fraser's eyes opened. "Oh. You," he whispered.

"He fell," Abby said. "There was old shrapnel. I took it out and he seemed—but he's worse today."

"Old shrapnel," Alma said, in a voice like the low

register of a fiddle. Abby and her grandmother exchanged alarmed looks.

"His name is Fraser," Abby said somewhat overloudly. "He's a Pinkerton detective, Mummy, he's not—"

"Abby," her mother interrupted. "Get some of the apples that have started to rot."

Abby made a funny, strained grimace at Grandma Collins, wrenched open a door Phin hadn't noticed, and thundered down the cellar stairs.

"Apples," Fraser said.

"Rotten apples draw out poison. It'll be all right, don't worry. This time it'll be all right."

Grandma Collins came behind her daughter-in-law, gently removing her shawl and burdens. She put her hands on the broad shoulders a moment.

Then Abby was back with a basin full of apples, brown and mushy, but still whole. They smelled sharp and cidery.

Abby began mashing them. Her mother bent over Fraser, tenderly unfastening his bandages. Fraser watched her hands.

"Alma?" The stranger, Brinkley, approached the blankets. "Should I stay? Or send the constable?"

She turned blankly. "Whatever for?"

"The constable," Abby said, mashing on. "That's a good idea, Phin, don't you think?"

Alma Collins looked at him over her shoulder. "That's the boy—what?" She bent to listen to Fraser, but Mr. Brinkley stared hard at Phin.

"Wouldn't it help to get the constable?" Abby asked Phin. "He could arrest Plume—don't *look* like that, Phin, he's a *blacksmith*! He lifts *ponies* off the ground—"

"Is Plume that feller came off the train?" Brinkley asked. " 'Cause he's headed this way."

Everyone in the room seemed suddenly distant to Phin, as if they'd zoomed ten feet away. Brinkley continued. "Passed him on the way up—he's driving Doc's buggy."

And Abby, looking pale, said, "Passed him how? Your horse is no faster than the doctor's."

"Thought you'd be glad of a warning. Alma'd nodded off, or I wouldn't have. I give him wrong directions. Sent him up to the old Larborough place."

Abby turned from her apples. Her eyes met Phin's. "It's an abandoned farm," she said. "It'll take him about half an hour to find that out and get back to the road. And I think he's going to be angry."

Phin had already faced it. There was only one reason Plume was coming here, and only one thing to do.

"If you could wait . . . a little while," he said to Brinkley, "I'll go down and meet him."

27
BLOOD MONEY

Abby said, "Oh Phin, no!" At the same moment her grandmother said, "Nonsense! You stay right here!"

Brinkley said, "Isn't this boy a murderer?"

"No, the man you passed is the murderer," Abby said. "Neither of you can go."

"I have to," Phin said. "He can't come here."

"He's one man. There are"—she looked around the room—"six of us."

Phin looked, too, at Brinkley's kind, bewildered face, Grandma Collins, Alma and Fraser looking deep into each other's eyes. Abby herself. Which of them would he risk?

He crossed to Fraser's blankets and crouched there. Slowly Fraser's eyes shifted to look at him.

"Plume's coming," Phin said. "I'm going down to meet him."

The old keenness sharpened Fraser's gaze. "Hide," he whispered. "I'll say I lost you."

"If he doesn't believe that—" Phin couldn't continue, couldn't put into words the pictures in his mind.

Fraser glanced at the woman bending over him, and his face changed. He lifted the hand on his uninjured side, flexing it oddly—looking for his derringer, Phin thought. With an angry grimace he let the hand fall.

"You have a plan, lad?"

"Not much of one," Phin said. His lips were numb. "Give him back his money—"

Fraser shook his head. "That's not what he wants."

Phin felt the bottom drop out of his stomach. The paper. Of course, the paper.

Abby came with the bowl of apples and fell to her knees beside her mother. Her face was white and knobby and fierce, strained to silence. Alma, as if all else was a dream, dipped her hands into the brown apple soup and spread it on Fraser's wound. His breath whistled. He looked at her again, holding her eyes like a lifeline.

But after a moment he whispered, "Gun. In my bags."

Phin shrugged helplessly. "Can't shoot."

"Then . . . why are you going? Throw yourself away?"

"I wonder that myself," Abby said in a choked voice.

I don't want to be killed in front of you. Phin couldn't say that. He didn't want to be killed at all, but to have Abby see it . . . He looked away from her, and caught Fraser watching him.

"Take the horse," Fraser said. "Draw him off. When you've lost him . . . come back."

"Your prisoner?" Phin managed.

"My *horse*," Fraser said. He reached up and they gripped hands. Fraser's was dry and warm and firmer than Phin had expected, more full of life. He gave Phin a strong look, a short, sharp nod. "You'll do fine, lad. See you in a bit."

Phin got up quickly, wondering if the man believed that. Fraser's long coat hung on a peg by the door. Phin took it down, releasing a dark reek of old blood. The left side lapel and shoulder were stiff with it. He shrugged into the garment, put on the hat. It fit, almost too tightly. Behind him Brinkley said, "He's just a boy. Shouldn't I—"

Phin stepped out the door and closed it on the argument. It opened immediately, and he knew Abby had followed. "Why did you take his coat?" she asked.

"Cold," Phin said. He couldn't tell her the real reason.

"I'll bring the mare in," she said in a tight voice.

Phin went with her to the barn, and took the bridle from its peg. He buckled the bit in and tied rope to the rings to make reins.

Outside he heard oats rattle in a wooden measure, a distant nicker, the sound of hooves. He stepped out the door as the horses came around the corner.

They made a beautiful pair; the mare deep-bodied, long and capable, marred only by her halting step, the stallion all spring and silk and velvet. Phin looped the reins around his neck. "Ho."

The stallion lowered his head into the folds of Fraser's coat. Three puffs of breath; then he looked past Phin at the house. In the delicate skin above the nostril, Phin saw again that strange purling of—what? Blood? Air? Spirit?

The horse turned his head toward the road. He gazed, or stretched with another sense toward something that commanded his attention.

Hurry, then. Phin reached up with the bridle. The stallion seemed to bow slightly, allowing him to put it on while still watching the road. Abby brought the saddle. Phin settled it and cinched it on.

"We're not helpless," Abby said suddenly. "We could do something."

"We're not like him," Phin said. That was the only way; wait in ambush, shoot Plume down as he drove into the yard. Plume would do that. Fraser might. None of the rest of them could.

He took the roll of money from his pocket, peeled off two bills, and handed them to Abby. She shook her head.

"No," Phin said. "It's—" It was blood money, probably, pay for Engelbreit's murder. Let a little of it go for something good. "It's board," he said. "If I come back—I'd like to stay awhile."

Abby listened; listened past when he stopped speaking, searching his face with her eyes. Then she did take the money, and surprised him with a quick, fierce hug, hard enough to hurt.

"*When* you come back, you're welcome to stay, and read all winter if you want. Be smart, Phin!" She turned away untying her apron, caught the mare with it, and they disappeared into the barn.

The stallion swung around, ready to follow. "Ho," Phin said, and mounted. With a hard lump swelling in his throat, he adjusted the clumsy rope reins, and touched his heels to the stallion's sides.

The motion beneath him was as he'd remembered, swift and smooth and almost too powerful. He circled, trying to get in synch, get the horse pointed where he meant to go.

He rode by the house. Grandma Collins came out on the step. Phin raised his hand stiffly, like a salute, and passed out of the yard into the shadowed road. Stone walls glided by. Tree trunks rippled. Bright leaves twirled down and Phin heard them land, whispering.

How calm he felt, how blank. His mind should be racing, planning, but it wouldn't. He was simply here, simply now. Maybe this was all courage amounted to, what Engelbreit felt, turning from his stove. Ah! Now this.

Was he afraid?

He was. Like stepping into empty air over the Dog Hole; something impossible was happening. He doubted he'd survive.

Yet he felt large, too, expanded to fill out Fraser's coat. He'd laid Fraser low, hadn't he? Lower than he meant, but he had done it.

The gravestones came into view in their straggling rows, the wet grass long and rank between them. A streak of snow remained in the cold shadow of the north wall, patterned with red leaves. It took Phin back in a rush to his mother's grave and Bittsville.

How quick they'd been to help in what ways they could, Murray and the Lundy's, Jimmy and Dennis. People were kind, people were brave. How many would be caught in Fraser's cave-in? Justice was never perfect. The innocent suffered with the guilty—and not all those Phin loved were good.

The stallion's ears sharpened. His steps faltered, and in a moment Phin, too, heard hoofbeats. A dark shape came into view below the graveyard: a buggy pulled by a brown horse.

Phin's hand on the reins checked the stallion for a heartbeat. The buggy came on without hesitation. At this distance Plume saw Fraser, as Phin had meant him to. Before he could look harder, and see Phin Chase, Phin kissed to the stallion and rode briskly up to the buggy.

Plume frowned in puzzlement. Then an ugly light flared in his eyes. He reached onto the seat beside him, and suddenly a gun was in his hand. The stallion wheeled. Phin grabbed for mane as the gun roared and the air hissed and the horse spun and he flew from the saddle.

He came down on leather again, hauling in the loose rope reins and whirling the stallion, whirling again as the doctor's terrified horse plunged past. The buggy careened toward the graveyard wall, bumping over the grass, and tipped on two wheels in the ditch.

A black shape leaped from it; Plume, landing clumsily in the road. His ankle turned. He fell heavily on one shoulder and came up with the gun pointing straight at the stallion's chest.

"Right there! Or I drop him."

"Ho," Phin said. He felt the horse dance under him, on the edge of disobeying. "Ho!"

Plume rose; awkward now, lame, but the gun never wavered. "Get down. Be a shame to miss and hurt him."

Phin didn't move. Plume shrugged and raised the gun, then hesitated. "Happened to the mule man?"

Phin jerked his chin backward, seeing what he wanted Plume to see—a body stretched out on the forest floor, no threat to anyone. "He was a Pinkerton agent." His voice worked. That surprised him.

"Was he?" Plume said. "Was he, now?" His eyes widened, with an inward look; thinking of things he'd said to Fraser, and of people Fraser had talked with back in Bittsville.

After a moment, though, he returned to the present, looking Phin over. The passion had died out of his face. He was pale and sober in all senses, with new lines beside his eyes. "I've never killed a kid," he said. "If you don't want to be the first, tell me and tell me quick. Where is it?"

"Your paper."

"My paper, as you call it. And don't pretend you can't read. Didn't I see you at Engelbreit's with a big book open in front of you? Hand it over."

Phin shook his head. "It's gone."

The gun muzzle twitched.

"I burned it," Phin said. As he said that, his gut fluttered, and he heard Engelbreit behind him at the stove crumpling newspaper, kindling his breakfast fire. He never got the chance to lay a chunk of wood on it. It must have flared and burned out while Plume was pushing the books off the shelf and Phin was running, and Fraser, unbeknownst, was picking up the fallen jacket. . . .

"Tell me you didn't read it," Plume said. "Tell me I don't have to kill you."

Did he want Phin to beg? Or did he mean it? The stallion pawed; Phin stroked the silken neck, soothingly. "I grew up in Murray's," he said. "I know better than to mess with Sleeper business."

"So you didn't read it?" Plume's eyes bored into Phin's, round and dark like Jimmy's eyes, round and dark like the hole at the end of the gun muzzle.

"I didn't read it."

Plume sighed and shut his eyes a second. "Fine," he said. "Fine."

"Is . . . Margaret in trouble about it?"

Plume's eyes opened again, with an expression of acute dislike. "What do you think, kid? Think I ratted on her? Think I tried to throw off the blame?"

Phin shook his head no. No, he thought better of Plume than that, strangely enough. But Margaret might have said the wrong thing at Murray's. The wrong people might have heard. Sleepers didn't war on women or kids—he'd always heard that. But they didn't do killings on their home turf either, and Plume had. And if Plume had caught him in his first rage, he'd be dead now. The old truths didn't hold these days, and there were more troubles coming.

"Listen," he said, "something bad's going to happen." He'd come down here in Fraser's coat, on Fraser's horse, to get close enough to say this. "There's Pinkertons all over coal country. A big trap, Fraser said. Tell Murray and . . . take Margaret away."

Plume listened, tired, unsurprised. At the end he said, "Makes you think she'd go with me?"

It sounded like a statement, not a question, but Phin

answered. "She'd like to see the West. She told my mother once."

Plume weighed that, hefting the gun in his hand; turned slightly to one side now, pointing toward the sky. "I've made nothing but mistakes the past few days," he said. "This might be another. Where you heading?"

Phin shrugged. "Canada?" He was a better liar than Fraser.

Plume sucked at his front teeth a moment. "If they catch you . . . you'll talk?"

Phin saw Engelbreit's wide eyes, heard his head hit the stove. He clenched his jaw hard, and nodded.

Plume's gun hand turned. Almost as an experiment, it seemed, he pointed the weapon at Phin's chest.

Then he let it drop to his side. "Go," he said.

Didn't he want the horse? Phin had expected that, been prepared to give up the animal. "Don't you—" he said, "I mean—I have your money. . . ."

"You know what?" Plume said, in a voice of weary dislike. "Keep it. I want you to have what you need to go a long, long way!" He limped toward the buggy.

The stallion shook his head, pulling the reins through Phin's slack hand, and surged uphill, toward the farm and the mare. Dazed, Phin let himself be carried. Was this real?

Or would Plume shoot after all? His back awaited the bullet. His heart ached at the beauty around him; birdsong, bright leaves, the gray house looking down, raising its eyebrows. No shot came. What had he done? Warned a murderer, helped him escape. What would they think?

His mother brushed by. "Whoso would be a man, Phinny . . ."

He was above the graveyard now. He heard Lucky barking, and glimpsed the buggy coming down the road, a rifle poking out of it, the familiar blue of Abby's dress. They'd heard the shot. This was a rescue party. How would Plume react to that? Phin turned to look back.

Plume was at the capsized buggy. As Phin watched, he slashed the traces and led the doctor's horse from the shafts. He wrapped the reins around his fist and sliced them riding short, dropped the ends in the road.

Now he climbed onto the stone wall and slid onto the horse's back. As he reined around there was a moment when he faced uphill, faced Phin. He checked the horse, staring. Phin stared back.

Then he turned downhill, toward Bittsville and his own concerns.

Phin rode uphill to his.

HISTORICAL NOTE

In the 1870s the coal-mining region of Pennsylvania was torn by strife. In response to union organizing among the miners—mainly Irish—the mine owners organized, too. They created a private militia, the Coal and Iron Police, and hired the Pinkerton Detective Agency to infiltrate the unions. In 1875, when their preparations were complete, they provoked a strike by drastically cutting wages.

The Long Strike lasted six months. Families went hungry, and leaders on both sides were murdered.

The strike failed. Violence continued and was blamed on the secret organization most commonly known as the Molly Maguires, or sometimes—as in this story—the Sleepers.

The Molly Maguires trace back to pre-Famine Ireland, when an armed group of that name resisted English occupation. In America from the 1850s on, every crime committed by an Irishman was blamed on the Molly Maguires. They were alleged to control the unions and the benevolent society, the Ancient Order of Hibernians—the AOH. Because of the group's secrecy, these charges remain impossible to prove. They may be anti-Irish, anti-Catholic, and anti-union propaganda, or they may be true. Or the truth may lie somewhere between.

The fact remains that organized violence did occur. Unfair mine bosses frequently received what was known as a "coffin notice," a death threat decorated with a hand-drawn black coffin. If the boss didn't leave, he was murdered.

Killings accelerated in the months after the Long Strike. Two mine officials were shot in the first weeks of September alone. Suspects were arrested, and later that year one of them, a miner named Jimmy Kerrigan, turned state's evidence.

Also in September James McParlan, a Pinkerton spy working undercover, delivered to his bosses a list of all known Molly Maguire members in coal country. The Pinkerton agency gave the names, as well as lists of alleged

Molly crimes, to a vigilante group that later attacked a home and murdered a suspect and his sister.

In March 1876 James McParlan's identity was discovered and he fled. He surfaced during the trial of five Molly Maguires for the murder of a policeman. His testimony and that of Jimmy Kerrigan resulted in the execution of twenty members of the organization. Others fled, and the organization was broken up.

Were they terrorists? Labor organizers? Thugs? Patriotic defenders of Irish rights? Accounts differ to this day.

Controversy also continues about the role of the Pinkertons. The Pinkerton National Detective Agency was founded in 1850 by Scottish immigrant Allan Pinkerton. Pinkerton had fled Scotland after taking part in a demonstration for workers' rights. In America the agency he founded became an arm of big business—mines, banks, railroads—and the United States government. Pinkerton was known among criminals as "the Eye," because of the agency's logo, an open eye with the motto "We never sleep." The term "private eye" originates with the Pinkerton Agency.

The FBI—Federal Bureau of Investigation—was modeled on Pinkerton's methods, which were innovative and aggressive. The American public first became aware of this side of the agency's work when Pinkerton detectives bombed the home of Jesse James's mother, wounding the elderly woman and killing a child but leaving the outlaw unscathed. This defeat was still rankling Pinkerton at the time of the Molly Maguire investigations and contributed to his determination to succeed. Many consider James McParlan, famous for his undercover work among the Molly Maguires, to have been a provocateur, instigating crimes for which members of the organization were later hanged. Certainly he knew in advance of at least two murders and did nothing to stop them. In his defense, his own life was at risk throughout the investigation, and there may have been nothing he could do.

There is no record of Pinkerton agents using tracking horses. I'm not aware of anyone doing so until recent years when horses came into use for search and rescue operations. But the scenting ability of horses has been observed and used by people for centuries, limited only by the human imagination.

Bittsville is a fictional coal town set in the anthracite region of Pennsylvania, between Wilkes-Barre and Pottsville. No person in the story is meant to represent a historical figure.

BIBLIOGRAPHY

Coleman, J. Walter. *The Molly Maguire Riots: Industrial Conflict in the Pennsylvania Coal Region.* New York: Arno & the New York Times, 1969.

Korsen, George. *Minstrels of the Mine Patch: Songs and Stories of the Anthracite Industry.* Hatboro, Pennsylvania: Folklore Associates, Inc., 1964.

Miller, Donald L., and Richard E. Sharpless. *The Kingdom of Coal: Work, Enterprise, and Ethnic Communities in the Mine Fields.* Philadelphia: University of Pennsylvania Press, 1985.

Nowacki, Terry. *The Air Scenting Horse: A New Concept for Search and Rescue,* 2001. www.airscentinghorse.com.

Trachtman, Paul, and the Editors of Time-Life Books. *The Gunfighters.* New York: Time-Life, 1974.

Wallace, Anthony F.C. Saint Clair. *A Nineteenth-Century Coal Town's Experience with a Disaster-Prone Industry.* Ithaca and London: Cornell University Press, 1981, 1985, 1987.

Special thanks to Jay Callahan and Paul Ziesmer for the loan of materials.